BEACON STREET GIRLS

This book belongs to:

VERITAS AMICITIA GAUDIUM
truth friendship fun!

BEACON STREET GIRLS

Be sure to read all of our books:

BSG Special Adventure Books:

BEACON STREET GIRLS

Freestyle with Avery

BY
ANNIE BRYANT

ALADDIN M!X

NEW YORK   LONDON   TORONTO   SYDNEY

ALADDIN M!X

An imprint of Simon & Schuster Children's Publishing Division
1230 Avenue of the Americas, New York, NY 10020
First Aladdin M!X edition December 2009
Copyright © 2007 by B*tween Productions, Inc.,
Home of the Beacon Street Girls.
Beacon Street Girls, KGirl, B*tween Productions, B*Street, and the characters Maeve, Avery, Charlotte, Isabel, Katani, Marty, Nick, Anna, Joline, and Happy Lucky Thingy are registered trademarks of B*tween Productions, Inc.
All rights reserved, including the right of reproduction in whole or in part in any form.
ALADDIN is a trademark of Simon & Schuster, Inc., and related logo is a registered trademark of Simon & Schuster, Inc.
ALADDIN M!X and related logo are registered trademarks of Simon & Schuster, Inc.
For information about special discounts for bulk purchases, please contact Simon & Schuster Special Sales at 1-866-506-1949 or business@simonandschuster.com.
The Simon & Schuster Speakers Bureau can bring authors to your live event. For more information or to book an event contact the Simon & Schuster Speakers Bureau at 1-866-248-3049 or visit our website at www.simonspeakers.com.
Designed by Dina Barsky
The text of this book was set in Palatino Linotype.
Manufactured in the United States of America
4 6 8 10 9 7 5 3
Library of Congress Control Number 2008939757
ISBN 978-1-4169-6435-3
ISBN 978-1-4169-9832-7 (eBook)

Who's Who

BSG

Katani Summers
a.k.a. Kgirl . . . Katani has a strong fashion sense and business savvy. She is stylish, loyal & cool.

Avery Madden
Avery is passionate about all sports and animal rights. She is energetic, optimistic & outspoken.

Charlotte Ramsey
A self-acknowledged "klutz" and an aspiring writer, Charlotte is all too familiar with being the new kid in town. She is intelligent, worldly & curious.

Isabel Martinez
Her ambition is to be an artist. She was the last to join the Beacon Street Girls. She is artistic, sensitive & kind.

Maeve Kaplan-Taylor
Maeve wants to be a movie star. Bubbly and upbeat, she wears her heart on her sleeve. She is entertaining, friendly & fun.

Ms. Razzberry Pink
The stylishly pink proprietor of the Think Pink boutique is chic, gracious & charming.

Marty
The adopted best dog friend of the Beacon Street Girls is feisty, cuddly & suave.

Happy Lucky Thingy and alter ego Mad Nasty Thingy
Marty's favorite chew toy, it is known to reveal its alter ego when shaken too roughly. He is most often happy.

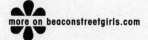
more on beaconstreetgirls.com

Part One
Snurf Madness!

"Telluride, here I come!"

1

Snurfer Dreams

I know what you're thinking," I said to my snake Walter as I gently placed him back in his cage. "This room is craaaaaazy." Frogster the frog hopped in his terrarium to show he agreed with my opinion. Normally my room was a certified disaster area—clothes, books, and sports stuff everywhere. But tonight, there wasn't a single piece of clothing on my floor, and I had put away all my equipment very neatly. (Okay, more like shoved it under my bed, but close enough, right?) Best of all, my suitcases were packed, zipped, and waiting for me by the door. I couldn't believe it. In twelve hours I'd be on a plane soaring over the city of Boston. That meant sixteen hours till Dad, and about thirty-six hours till I'd be hitting the primo Colorado snowboarding slopes in Telluride. "Yup, definitely crazy."

I signed online to say a vacation good-bye to my best friends, the BSG.

Chat Room: BSG

File Edit People View Help

4kicks: hey! the Ave has landed. what's up?
Kgirl: there u r.
lafrida: all ready 2 go?
4kicks: finally. Scott & I sorta had a tomato sauce war so I had to do 2 loads of laundry
Kgirl: bet your mom loooved that
4kicks: I wouldn't say loooved, but she's in a good mood now
flikchic: she's gonna miss u 2 so much, I bet
4kicks: here's the big thing—Scott's not coming
lafrida: no way! y not?
4kicks: he's going to this culinary school thing in NYC
la frida: so ur going 2 CO alone? r u scared?
4kicks: not really. I'm waaay psyched 4 this.
flikchic: I don't know how you travel alone ... when I'm rich and famous, I'll def need personal assistants for planes!
4kicks: but I'm not alone ... didn't U tell, Char?
skywriter: no ... I thought u'd want 2

5 people here

4kicks
Kgirl
lafrida
flikchic
skywriter

4kicks: Marty is flying with me. LOL
lafrida: ur sooo lucky!
Kgirl: write us the minute u get there?
4kicks: haha not THE minute but I will that nite
flikchic: u better!!
skywriter: we'll have a sleepover ASAP when u come back.
4kicks: thanks for letting Marty go with me.

btw—thanks sooo much 4 the package!
skywriter: ur saving it 4 the plane ride, rite???
4kicks: yes but it's hard! OK I gtg to bed! big day ...
flikchic: OK! have fun!
lafrida: sleep tight.

Sleep? Hah! I jumped into bed and fidgeted around under the covers. Sleep was pretty much the last thing on my mind that night. What *was* on my mind? Well, that was easy. Let's see ... the Snurfer, the Snurfer, and oh, yeah, the Snurfer. I'd been thinking about the first annual Telluride Snurfer Snowboarding Competition for months.

Snurfer might sound like a funny name for a snowboarding competition, but this was totally legit— named after the very first snowboard ever created!

Waaaaay back in 1965, a dude named Sherman Poppen tied a couple of skis together so his daughter could sled standing up. Only instead of "snowboard" (a word that hadn't been invented yet—duh!), his wife decided to call it a "snurfer"—a combination of "snow" and "surfer." I think it's pretty cool that the very first snowboard was custom-made by this girl's dad, just for her.

My dad, who owns a ski shop in Colorado, organized the Snurfer Competition in Telluride this year, and it was going to be *huge*. I'm talking pro athletes and movie stars. I had imagined how cool it would be for both my big bro Scott and I to place in the Snurfer top ten . . . especially in a contest that Dad was running. Of course, with Scott going to this fancy-schmancy culinary school thing instead, that idea was totally out the door. Now that I was going to be representing the Maddens all by myself in the Snurfer, I was doubly determined to win it.

But I was feeling less sure about doing all the other parts of the trip by myself. Who was I supposed to hang out with? Who was going to show me where to go in the airports? Especially switching planes in Denver. I hadn't flown alone in a long time. How was I supposed to know which gate was mine? But Mom promised me that the airline's "unaccompanied minor program" would work out just fine—I'd have a flight attendant with me during all the tricky parts. Plus I was taking "the little dude"—The Marty Man himself—with me, so that would make it better. Marty, our little adopted dog, lived with Charlotte, but she thought he would enjoy a trip to Colorado with me.

But there was one more thing . . . the thing I thought was the strangest of all. Dad wrote me an e-mail just a few days ago telling me that there had been some changes in his life. What was that supposed to mean? Mom knew something about it too, I was almost positive. She said that on this trip I should be prepared to meet some of Dad's new friends, but no matter what she was sure they'd be very nice. Very nice? Dad's old friends seemed plenty nice already. It was all *very* . . . mysterious.

I squeezed my eyes shut and tried not to keep wondering what this big trip would be like. I just had one rule—no matter what, it would be an adventure. For some reason, adventure had a habit of following me. Or maybe it was the other way around.

I rolled over, pulled my comforter up to my chin, and whispered, "Night, Walter. Ribbet, Frogster. Sleep tight." I set my alarm clock for six a.m. Less than twelve hours till take off. Telluride, here I come!

CHAPTER

2

Chicken Salad Air

I love it when airplanes race down the runway—I get a rush the moment the wheels lift off the pavement. Today I had a window seat, so I got to watch the little houses and buildings in Boston getting smaller and smaller. Pretty soon the city looked like a tiny town filled with itsy-bitsy people. I smiled. Somewhere down there in tiny Boston were my family, my house, and my four best friends! I couldn't believe I'd ever been nervous about taking this trip by myself.

Another awesome part of flying is that you get to soar through the clouds and shoot out *above* them. Even though it was a cold, rainy morning in Boston, above the clouds it was sunny and clear blue all around. The bad weather was below us—too cool!

Four and a half hours and one movie later, Marty and I landed in Denver and boarded the next plane to Telluride. I took a deep breath and relaxed. Next stop . . . Dad's! It was the perfect time to open my present from the BSG. I pulled the brightly wrapped package out of my carry-on bag. I couldn't wait to see what was inside. I had just started to tear into the wrapping when a woman across the aisle suddenly asked me, "Does your dog like flying?"

She leaned forward to get a peek at Marty in his carrier, tucked under the seat in front of me. Her perfume smelled like when you first walked into a department store. "Look at the pwecious widdew cutie patootie. Hello handsome. Awen't you da cootest widdew puppy!" If my brothers were here we all would've been holding the laughter in. What language was this woman speaking, anyway?

"He's not really a pup—" I began to explain, but just then Marty started practically singing from his carrier!

"Ooow, oow, oow . . ." he yodeled.

The woman got so excited she began to clap. "What a little darling!" she whispered to me. "Who's the cootest widdew baby?" she gushed.

Ick. Thank goodness Marty wasn't wearing one of those doggy sweaters my friend Maeve likes so much. Then we would've *really* been in trouble.

I reached into my bag and gave Marty his favorite chew toy, Happy Lucky Thingy, a pink little dude who's smiling on one side and frowning on the other. It used to be mine when I was a baby. With his mouth full of Happy Lucky, Marty's serenade was pretty much over, and the woman across the aisle leaned back in her seat and picked up a magazine. Finally!

Now I could concentrate on opening my present. First, I unwrapped a key ring with tiny charms of a snowboard, a soccer ball, and a small froggie pen. The note attached read: "Have fun, Avery . . . *WRITE POSTCARDS!* Love, Charlotte." I knew the second small package was from Katani before I even read the card. A fleece navy blue ear warmer with a snowflake design—that was totally a Kgirl original. Katani was amazing at designing clothes. Even though I never paid too much attention to fashion, I could tell that this ear warmer might look cool when I was boarding down the mountain. Maeve made me a mix CD. For a second I was afraid that it would be filled with Maeve's favorite show tunes, but I was wrong. She had put on a bunch of awesome songs—mostly pop and some classic rock. The last thing was a mini-collage of all the BSG . . . from Isabel, of course. Her art was so good that I was sure people would buy it in a store someday. But this collage was way too special to be sold in a store—it was just for me. *My friends are the coolest!* I thought. *How lucky am I?*

"Miss the BSG yet, Marty?"

Marty started to make little whimpering, whining sounds. He was totally sick of the carrier. "I know how you feel, little dude." I always felt really cooped up after sitting at a desk all day at school.

The loudspeaker above me made a crackling noise, and the pilot's voice came on. "We're now approaching Telluride Regional Airport, the highest commercial airport in the United States, 9,078 feet above sea level. Take a look out the windows, because this is one of the best views in San Miguel County. We might hit a little turbulence coming in, so fasten your seat belts. We'll be landing in about ten minutes."

The Telluride landing seemed more like a cool ride at an amusement park than what it was: a tiny plane navigating through the huge San Miguel Mountain Range. I took a deep breath as the turbulence grabbed us and shook the plane. "Hang on, Marty!" I warned.

Marty began to yowl in a voice I'd never heard before. Poor little guy was nervous. And he wasn't the only one. The woman across the aisle—the baby-talker—grabbed the armrests on either side of her.

"Oxygen!" she panted. "Where are the masks? It's a real *emergency*."

The other people on the plane looked more confused than worried.

"Hey, is this your first time going to Telluride?" I asked her.

She put her hand over her heart. "Yes. Why do you ask?" Her face was white.

"Well, because this can happen when you go through the Rockies on a small plane. You don't have to worry," I told her.

The woman looked at me suspiciously. "B-b-but the plane . . . it's sh-sh-shaking so hard!" she protested. "I've never been on a plane that shakes and bounces this much!" Marty's little howls told me whose side he was on. Hmm . . . I'd have to speak to that "little dude" about loyalty!

"No, that's just the turbulence the pilot was talking about. Believe me, it's completely normal." Then I thought of something. When I was younger, Scott always used to tell me jokes through this part of the ride to distract me. Unfortunately, the only jokes I could remember were about snowboarding. Seeing this woman with gray hair pulled into a tight bun and a light blue silk dress with matching blue sparkly shoes, well, she didn't really seem like the snowboarding type. But still, it was worth a shot.

"Hey, how do you get a snowboarder off your porch?" I asked her.

"Pardon?"

"How do you get a snowboarder off your porch?" I repeated, smiling.

She shook her head. "How?"

"Pay for the pizza."

The corners of her dark red lipsticked mouth curled into a smile.

"How do snowboarders introduce themselves?" I asked and didn't wait for her to guess before I blurted, "Ohhh . . . sorry, duuuuude!"

She cracked up laughing. "My nephew is a boarder. And that is exactly how he talks!" She chuckled. The plane had calmed down a bit and now the woman glanced outside. "Oh my!" She gasped. "It's simply breathtaking!"

"I know," I said. Flying through the Rockies made me feel ten times bigger and ten times smaller at the exact same time. The big feeling came from something I could only describe as freedom. Back in Brookline, I was always around cars and buildings and people in lines waiting to pay for groceries. In the summer, when I'd go camping with Dad and my bros in Colorado, it was really cool just how far away we could get from all the craziness of the real world. The small feeling definitely came from the fact that the Rocky Mountains are absolutely gigantic! They looked like shark teeth blown up and stretched to infinity.

The plane smoothed out as we came in for a landing. The wheels bumped when we hit the runway, and Marty gave a little "Yip!" As we taxied toward the airport buildings, I wondered what this trip had in store.

I was the first one off the plane, down the steps, and onto the tarmac. Marty trotted along beside me as fast as his little legs could move. My rolling carry-on bag bumped and bounced as we flew across the pavement. The cold air felt fresh against my cheeks. Suddenly the "little dude" stopped. Oops . . . a little time for some doggy business. It was a long ride. Whatever.

"Huh. I didn't remember these doors being automatic!" I said as I pushed them open and Marty and I rushed into the airport. I looked around for Dad, but he was nowhere to be seen. *Oh no!* This was just what I was afraid of. Then I noticed the man who had been holding the door open. He was wearing a huge fleece jester hat with the word "Snurfman" printed across the front in bright blue.

3

Blindsided

Dad!" I jumped into his arms and gave him the biggest hug ever. "I missed you so much!" I told him.

"I missed you too, Ave!" he said, swinging me around. There was nothing like a Dad superhug. "But I just have one question . . . how much did you grow since I last saw you? One foot? Two?" He placed me on the ground and grabbed his back like he'd pulled a muscle.

"Ha, ha, very funny, Dad." I knew I hadn't grown a foot . . . barely even a couple of inches. But it still felt good that Dad pretended.

"Excuse me?"

We turned around. It was the woman in the blue dress from the plane.

She smiled at Dad. "I just wanted to tell you that you have a lovely daughter. You should be very proud of this young lady." Then she bent down and rubbed Marty's back. "I dust wuv this widdew wuv button!"

Dad gave me a look that said he *was* very proud as the woman walked away.

"Now is this the little wuv button?" Dad asked, pointing to Marty. "Your mom told me he was supposed to be your guard dog."

"You bet he is!" I picked up Marty to make the introductions. "Dad, Marty. Marty, Dad."

Dad shook Marty's paw. "Pleased to make your acquaintance, Marty. I've heard so much about you."

"He's heard all about you too." I put Marty down and he stood up on his hind legs and started leading the way toward the exit, being a showoff in his typical Marty way. "He's perfect, most of the time." I told Dad about Marty freaking out during the turbulence as we grabbed my suitcase and headed for Dad's big, white van—the official Snurfmobile. The door of the Snurfmobile had the ATS Sports logo printed on it. ATS, the name of Dad's store, stood for Avery-Tim-Scott—the three most rockin' boarders in Colorado, naturally!

"You think you got enough stickers on this thing?" I joked. The bumper sticker situation on Dad's van was seriously out of control. The back door was almost completely covered with decals of snowboards, skis, canoes, and slogans like "Surf Colorado" and "The Snurfer Competition—Are you *shreddy*?"

"Welcome to Snurfer Central. And are *you* totally shreddy, Ave?"

"I'm shreddy for sure! Number one, baby!" I could hardly wait for the competition.

Dad smiled. "That's my girl. But remember, Ave . . . this Snurfer thing is just for fun, right?"

"Duh! Of course," I answered. *And to win!* I added to myself. Dad always said that the number-one rule about sports was to have fun. He was right, obviously, but that didn't mean winning was *against* the rules.

Dad loaded up the trunk and slammed the back door. I automatically shouted, "Shotgun!" and bolted to the front seat. It took a split second for me to remember that I didn't need to call shotgun at all. Scott, the other front seat grabber, was way back in Boston.

"It's weird without Scott here. I miss him already, don't you?" I asked.

"Well, of course," Dad said as he started the van. "I miss you guys all the time. But this culinary school is a big honor for your brother. And . . ." He turned the van toward town. "I'm looking forward to having quality time with my favorite daughter."

"Hey . . . I'm your only daughter!"

"But still my favorite." Dad laughed.

We headed down Keystone Hill on the road that led right onto Telluride's main street. "Okay. Is it time?" he asked, placing his finger on the CD power button.

As soon as we hit Colorado Avenue (which all the Telluride locals—including me, of course!—call Main Street), I gave Dad the thumbs-up and he pressed play. John Denver's voice filled the van: *"He was born in the summer of his twenty-seventh year, comin' home to a place he'd never been before . . ."* We cruised down Main Street, and Dad and I belted out "Rocky Mountain High." It was our ritual for the official beginning of a Telluride vacation. I hugged Marty close, hoping he wouldn't start howling again, this time at the off-key noises coming from Dad and me. Neither of us could carry a tune, but that never stopped us from singing . . . or trying to, anyway.

I always had to catch my breath when I saw the eye-popping, jaw-dropping scene ahead. Snow covered most of the buildings in town with a blanket of white, and behind them rose the huge peaks of the mountains. Once, when I was showing Maeve pictures of Telluride, I convinced her that *The Sound of Music* was filmed there. (Maeve goes nuts over musicals.) She believed me, too . . . and then pummeled me with a pillow when she found out I was kidding. But Telluride really did look like some kind of movie backdrop. It was in a narrow valley surrounded by three massive, snow-covered mountain peaks: Ajax, Ballard, and Telluride Peak. Halfway down Main Street, on the right, I could see the ski gondola moving up the Telluride Ski Resort mountain to Mountain Village and the ski runs. I wanted to stop the car, grab a board, and ride up the mountain right then and there!

"First thing tomorrow, Ave." It was like Dad could read my mind sometimes.

Riding in the Snurfmobile was kind of like being famous. All the cars that passed honked at us and waved. Even people on the street stopped to salute my dad, the Snurfman, and he honked and waved right back. Dad's bumper sticker love was contagious . . . people knew that if they caught the Snurfman in the Snurfmobile, there was a good chance he might give them some sticker freebies. That, plus his friendliness, made Dad a pretty popular dude around these parts.

Marty put his paws against the window and barked at a German shepherd riding in a pickup truck beside us. Almost everyone in Telluride had a dog. "See, Marty? You fit right in!" I scratched Marty's head and he happily slurped my hand.

Dad pulled into his reserved space in front of ATS Sports. "I just have to run in here quickly. Do you want to come in, or stay in the—" I was out of the car before he had a chance to say it, and Dad laughed. "Okay, I guess that was a silly question."

I ran toward ATS with Marty snug in my arms. "*Come on,* Dad. Of course I want to see the store! What new stuff do you have? Any cool snowboarding gear? Oh! Is Bob working today? I can't wait to see Bob!"

When I burst through the doors, a blast of warm air hit me, along with the smell of leather, ski wax, and new gear. As I put Marty on the floor, I glanced around the store for Bob. A real live cowboy from Wyoming, Bob had been the assistant manager of Dad's store for as long as I could remember.

The only person in there wearing the official ATS T-shirt, though, was a pretty blond lady stocking up the hand warmers. "Where's Bob?" I asked Dad.

"Um . . ." Dad scratched his head. "Avery, Bob had to go back to Wyoming. I meant to tell you that over the phone, but it completely slipped my mind." That was strange. In all the conversations that I'd had with Dad over the last several weeks, how could he forget something as huge as Bob leaving?

"Wyoming? Why?" I wasn't really freaking out . . . I

was just expecting to see Bob leaning over the ATS counter like old times. What was happening here—first no Scott, and now no Bob?

"His son, Wallie, opened a new dude ranch and he wanted his dad to help out. And Bob was ready to go back. He missed his family." Dad put his arm around my shoulder. I got the message—it was hard to be far away from the people you loved.

The blonde lady came over with an armful of bright pink helmets. "Oof! These are heavy! Jake, that new catalog sent us more helmets in pink than I know what to do with!" She dropped them in a pile beside me and held out her hand. "Lemme guess. You're Avery!"

I shook her hand but I didn't get a chance to even say anything, because the woman kept talking. "I've heard so much about you!" she said. "Your dad's told me so many wonderful things. It's great to finally meet you." *Well, who is she?* I wondered. I hadn't heard anything about her before.

"Avery, this is Andie Walker. Andie's my new assistant manager," said Dad. I stared at the woman who grinned back at me. I could tell right away that she loved the slopes. Anybody with cheeks that tanned in the winter *had* to spend her days on the mountains. She was wearing jeans, but they were trendy jeans for someone my mom's age, and she had long, blonde hair pulled back with an elastic. Two points in my book . . . I was always a fan of rocking the ponytail.

"Nice to meet you," I said. "Sorry, I've never heard of you before."

"Avery!" Dad turned as pink as the helmets.

"What? It's true. . . ." I smiled at Andie to show I meant no hard feelings.

Andie laughed and Dad patted her on the back. "Everyone around here just loves Andie . . . I'm sure you will too Ave. She's a great addition to Telluride!" And then—was it just my imagination—or did Dad actually WINK at her? *No way*, I thought. But then—and I was positive about this—Andie winked back!

CHAPTER

4

Rolling Down the Windows

I have a daughter who's about your age," Andie Walker said. "Her name's Kazie, and she can't wait to meet you. She's a snowboarder too! I'm sure you guys will totally hit it off." Andie turned to Dad. "Jake, before I forget, what do you want us to bring over for dinner tomorrow?"

Ohhh! Dad was having a party . . . a welcome party for ME! That was definitely what the wink was for. I wondered who was invited besides Andie and her daughter Kazie. Hey, the more the merrier!

"I'll talk to you about it later," Dad said to Andie, and I pretended not to notice when he tilted his head in my direction. Wow, Dad was *way* bad at surprises.

I felt something tug my hand. It was Marty, trying his hardest to pull me outside the store and explore the streets of Telluride. "I know how you feel, Marty Man. Dad . . . can we go now?" I shifted on my feet. I loved the store, but I was more than ready to start having fun.

"All right, all right," he agreed.

"Oh, Jake, Donnie Keeler called about the Snurfer. His plane comes in tomorrow morning."

"DONNIE KEELER!" I exclaimed. "Donnie Keeler, the Golden Egg, is coming *here?*" Donnie Keeler is an amazing snowboarder on his way to the next Olympic Games. He already won the gold once, and according to every boarding magazine around, he's America's number-one hope for the next Games. They call him the Golden Egg because of his curly, bright yellow hair . . . and because of his *golden* all-star talent. Donnie Keeler is HUGE in the boarding world.

"Donnie Keeler's our celebrity judge for the competition," Dad said. He was trying to be cool, I could tell, but his eyes were shining. He turned to Andie. "Tell DK to give me a ring when he gets in. And I'll call *you* later."

"Sounds good. Nice to finally meet you, Avery," Andie said with a wave.

"Donnie Keeler . . ." I murmured and felt Dad poke my shoulder. "Ow! Nice to meet you too, Andie."

Dad and I walked out of ATS to the Snurfmobile. "Let's take Marty home and get him settled in. I got him a dish with his name on it," Dad said and jumped in the driver's seat.

"Is it all right if he sleeps with me?"

"I don't see why not."

"Thanks! I can't believe it . . . a whole week with Marty and you, Dad. This is unbelievable!"

"I noticed you mentioned Marty first. Guess I know where I stand." Dad grinned as he turned left into the driveway of our house.

Dad lived in the cutest gingerbread-style house at the corner of Willow and Columbia, east of the fire station, near the end of the canyon. I was glad that his place was on the sunny side of town—the north. In the winter, the mountains cast a shadow over the south side of Main Street. Even though we'd be closer to the gondola and the ski slopes if we lived on the south side, it was much colder. Besides, Telluride was so small that it was easy to walk.

The minute Dad stopped the van, I jumped out and ran inside. Marty followed behind me, barking all the way. I burst through the front door, stood in the hallway for a second, and took a deep breath. I loved the smell of Dad's house—all sorts of wood. There was the pine tree incense, the cedar closets, and best of all, the wood-burning fireplace. *Mmm! The smell of winter!*

The first thing I wanted to do was visit my room. "Come on, M-Dawg. I'm gonna give you the royal tour." I scooped up the little pooch and carried him upstairs.

Dad's house sort of reminded me of a tree house. There was a spiral staircase right in the middle of the family room, and the upstairs was all open so you could see the kitchen right from the hallway railing. My brothers' bedroom was across from mine and when we were little we made tin can phones to communicate.

"Check it out, Marty, Dad got you your very own dish, and one of those doughnut pillow beds. See, you can curl up right in the middle of it and be all cozy warm . . . only for naps though. Because guess who you get to sleep with? Yup, yours truly. And look at the toys. A ball and a tug-of-war rope." Marty went crazy over most of the new stuff—sniffing around his new bed and the dish. But the toys he left alone. One look and he turned around and stuck his nose in the air. Marty was a one-toy type of dog . . . and that toy was Happy Lucky Thingy.

Dad had gotten me big bins that rolled under the bed to put my things in. I didn't have to fold anything! I even had my own computer here. My favorite place in the room was my window seat that looked out on the mountain, the town, and the ski slopes. My blanket was folded right where I left it last summer. I placed Marty's pillow bed in the window seat so he could keep a lookout for me when I came back from the mountain.

I could tell right away that Marty felt at home. As soon as I put his poofy doughnut down he crawled right in, walked around it a few times, and snuggled up inside. He was sound asleep when Dad brought my suitcase into the room.

"I think Marty's a little tuckered out after his big day, Ave." Dad grinned. "Bet he's still getting used to the altitude change. It can be just as hard for dogs as for people."

I looked at Marty snoozing peacefully in his doughnut. "Yeah, usually he's a pretty high-energy dude."

"Kind of like someone else I know." Dad coughed and looked in my direction.

I shrugged. "Hey, speaking of high energy . . . I'm totally starving!"

Dad knew exactly what to do. "Ready for burgers?" he asked. Fat Alley Burgers made the best burgers in Telluride. I had been thinking about a big, juicy one ever since I got off the plane.

"I'm ready! Let's go." I started to charge out the door but Dad caught me on the way.

"Whoa, hold on a sec, Ave. It's freezing out there. A sweater might not be a bad idea, huh?" he suggested. "How 'bout we leave in five minutes. I'm going to call Bif and tell her you made it here safe and sound." Bif was Dad's nickname for my mom. Even though they were divorced, they were still friends. I was lucky that way.

"Fat Alley Burgers made the best burgers in Telluride."

"Tell her I say hi!" I yelled. I grabbed my favorite winter sweater from my suitcase. It was blue with white stripes going down the sleeves. The ear warmer Katani made me matched perfectly, so I wore that too. The outfit must have been kind of different from what I normally wear, because when I came downstairs Dad looked surprised.

"Wow, Avery. You look so . . . grown up," Dad said. "I like your headband."

"*Come on,* Dad. And FYI it's an *ear warmer*, okay?"

"No, really," he said. "Look at you here." Dad pointed to the picture of us over the mantel—a photograph taken four years ago that Dad had gotten blown up and framed. Dad, Tim, Scott, and I were standing at the top of Gold Hill, holding our snowboards. My smile was so huge that you could see I was missing three teeth. Later that day we got free chili at a stand by the chairlift and ate the whole bowl on our way up to the summit. The snow was totally perfect— "pow-pow" as we snowboarders would say. I remembered it like it was yesterday. And I knew that Dad was right . . . I definitely looked a lot older now. (Even if I was still a shortie.)

The air outside the diner was a combination of burgers, fries, and fresh snow. Dad and I breathed deeply before going in. "Best smell ever!" I declared.

The restaurant was toasty warm and full of people. "Avery Madden!" Tommy, one of the ski instructors, slapped me five. "Long time no see!" The best part of having a home away from home is seeing everyone again when you came back to visit.

His girlfriend, Kimberly, waved too. "Welcome back, Avery. Are you ready to Snurf?"

I loved that everyone in Telluride expected me to enter the competition. "I'm super psyched!" I said. "It's going to be shred-tastic."

"How's Bah-ston?" came a low voice from behind me. I turned around to see Charlie, a gondola operator at one of the stations in Telluride. His skin was permanently suntanned and leathery from being in the sun every day.

I tried to keep a straight face when I answered him. People who don't live in Boston just can't do the accent, but it was so funny to hear them try. "Boston's cool, Charlie. Not enough snow yet for shredding, though, that's for sure."

As usual, Robbie, the owner of Fat Alley, was there working the grill. When he saw us, he walked around the counter to give me a big hug. He smelled like grease and ketchup. "You ready for a Fat Alley special?" he asked.

"So ready." I hopped onto a spinning stool at the counter. When we were little, Scott and I used to spin around and around until we got so dizzy that we could barely stay on. It was a game that Dad wasn't crazy about. "Robbie, can you make mine a double cheeseburger with cheddar and bacon, please?" Dad called.

"You got it!" Robbie went back to the grill and waved his spatula. "And for you, Ave?"

"Burger with lettuce and tomato!" Dad nudged my foot with his and I added, *"Please."*

The waitress, Bonnie, walked over with three mugs on her tray. Bonnie was about my mom's age, maybe a little younger. She had short brown hair and always wore a pink-checkered dress—the Fat Alley uniform—and a warm, friendly smile. Bonnie and my dad had moved to Telluride about the same time. "Coffee for you, Jake. And for Avery . . . hot chocolate with extra marshmallows, hold the whipped cream."

I cupped my hands around the warm mug and breathed in the rich chocolate. "Mmm, mmm! Thanks, Bonnie. Do you know the drinks of like, everyone in the state of Colorado?"

Bonnie rolled her eyes. "Oh, goodness no! Only in San Miguel County." She poked Dad in the elbow. "So Jake, where is Andie, huh? I have her green tea here."

Dad's coffee must have gone down the wrong pipe, because he started coughing . . . *a lot.*

"She's closing up," I answered for him. "Andie's the lady I met at the store, right, Dad?"

Dad gulped his water. "Uh, yeah, Avery. So I guess no tea tonight, Bonnie. Thanks though."

Bonnie looked at Dad and me. "I better go finish up with . . . stuff," she said and bustled off.

"Weird. Why would Bonnie make tea if Andie isn't even here?" I asked Dad, then whispered, "Maybe she's getting a little, you know, *loco-loco* . . . ?"

Dad shifted in his seat and stared into his mug. He was being so weird! I decided it was to time to tell him the gig was up about his "surprise" party for me.

"Okay, Dad, what's up? Is this about my surprise party?"

"Surprise party?" asked Dad.

"*Dad*, I've already figured it all out. I heard you talking to Andie at the store . . . c'mon . . . she and Kazie coming over for dinner?"

Dad got a funny look on his face. He took a sip of coffee and played with his spoon. "Avery, there's no surprise party. It really is just Andie and Kazie coming over for dinner . . . a dinner party."

The excited smile slipped off my face, but I tried my very best to keep smiling, so Dad wouldn't know I was a teeny-tiny bit disappointed. (And a teeny-tiny bit embarrassed, too.) "Well don't you think we should invite Robbie and Bonnie and Kimberly? Ooh, and what about the other people who work at ATS? I mean, if we're having a dinner party and all?"

Dad sat up and looked me straight in the eye. "I need to talk to you about something. I've been *meaning* to talk to you, but I wanted to wait until you were here . . . in person. Avery, Andie isn't just the manager of my store." Dad took a deep breath. "Andie is the woman I'm seeing."

It took a moment for this news to sink in. "You mean, like, your *girlfriend*?" I said the word slowly. Hearing it sounded just as strange as saying it.

"I—I've been seeing Andie for some time, Avery. I like her a lot . . . and I hope that you'll like her too," Dad explained. I looked over at Tommy and Kimberly cuddling in their booth and suddenly pictured Dad and Andie doing the same thing. *WEIRD TO THE MAX.*

"Her daughter Kazie's a great boarder, just like you. I have a feeling you two will be best friends in no time," he added. I remembered the BSG and secretly thought, *I'm not really looking for any more best friends.*

"Does Mom know about Andie? Do Tim and Scott?"

Dad made an "iffy" face. "Well . . . I've told Mom, and she's totally fine with it. She said if I liked Andie, she was sure Andie was a nice person. But Tim and Scott don't know yet. Do you think I should tell them over the phone?"

I shrugged. "Whatever. If you want." How was I

supposed to know how to tell them? Was there a rule for this type of thing? Maybe he had to tell us because he wanted Andie to stick around for a long time. *How* long was the question. "So are you two going to get married or what?" I asked him.

Dad spewed coffee out of his mouth and all over the counter. He coughed and wiped himself off. "Avery, I've only been dating her for three months."

"So then you're *not*."

"Avery . . ." Dad was usually kind of a chatterbox like me. It was strange to see him like this . . . not really knowing what to say. Well that was okay. I didn't really know what to say either.

"Avery, I have no idea what the future will be. I like spending time with Andie. She's nice and fun to be with. Plus Kazie's a great kid. She works at the store on the weekends." *How many times is Dad going to bring up this Kazie character?* I wondered. I used to work at the store when I came to visit. Would Dad even need my help if he had Kazie around?

"Do you want to talk more about this, Ave?" asked Dad.

I looked at Dad like he was crazy. "Talk about it? Dad, the Snurfer Competition is only a few days away! Don't you think we have much more important things to talk about? Like what kind of jumps I should do, and what time we're going to hit the slopes tomorrow, and when I'm going to get to meet Donnie Keeler, and—"

"S'cuse me, Avery. Your burgers are all ready," Bonnie announced, sliding two plates in front of me and Dad.

The burgers were thick and juicy on homemade sesame buns. On each of our plates were a small mountain of potato wedges and a little bowl of coleslaw.

"This looks unbelievable, Bonnie. Another master-piece," Dad raved.

"Yeah, thanks," I chimed, but instead of digging in, I just stared at the burger. For some reason, I had suddenly lost my appetite.

I was tired out by the time we got back to Dad's. I showered, changed into my PJs, and snuggled up with Marty in my bed. Then I suddenly remembered what I'd promised my friends right before I left: an e-mail.

```
To: Charlotte, Katani, Maeve, Isabel
From: Avery
Subject: Hello from CO


Hey BSG! I miss you already. Telluride is a
snowboarder's heaven right now! Can't wait to
shred it up! Other big news—Dad has a new girl-
friend. Totally weird. She has a 13-year-old
daughter named Kazie who Dad says is an awesome
snowboarder, but I'll have to C it 2 believe it.
Marty traveled like a pro, except when the plane
hit turbulence. (But don't ask him about it—
don't want to embarrass the little dude!) BTW,
thank you guys tons for the presents. They rock!
TTYL,
Avery


PS—Guess who the celeb judge for the Snurfer
is ... give you 1 clue: THE GOLDEN EGG.
```

5

Crazie Kazie

I opened my eyes to a sunlit room, rolled over, and found something gray and furry right next to my face. It took a split second for me to realize that the fur ball was Marty and to remember why Marty was in my bed. I bolted upright. I was in Telluride. It was a perfectly good boarding day. I didn't have a second to lose!

I heard the crackling sound of bacon on the griddle. "Mmm, mmm," I said, sniffing the air. I could smell my dad's coffee, too. Thank goodness Dad and I were both early birds. When I looked over the upstairs railing, I spied Dad at the stove flipping banana pecan pancakes—his breakfast specialty. I tiptoed down the spiral staircase and snuck up behind him. "GOOD MORNING!" I sang loudly.

Dad jumped a little (not as much as I hoped!), but at least no pancakes went flying. "Hey there." He pointed to me with the spatula. "Didn't you learn your lesson after your last pancake fight with Scott?"

"Ha, ha . . . *never!*" I grabbed a plate holding a tall stack of pancakes.

Marty scampered downstairs and leaped onto the window seat. He nuzzled into the cushion and started people/dog watching, his nose steaming up the glass.

"I bet Marty'll make tons of friends here in Telluride," said Dad. "All he's gotta do is take a walk around the block, and he'll have himself a dog-fest."

I drizzled a zigzag of syrup on my pancake pile. "Um, no offense, Dad, but Marty doesn't need to make more friends. He's got a whole dog posse back home. And a poodle girlfriend."

"Is that a fact?"

I gulped down a mouthful of pancake. "Sure is. He's the coolest pup in town! You miss La Fanny, Marty?" I asked.

Marty barked, but I wasn't sure if it was a "yes" or a "holla!" to the Colorado dogs outside the window.

"Are you going to take the day off to go snowboarding with me, Dad?"

Dad sat down at the table with me. "You bet! I was thinking we'd head up to Mountain Village after breakfast. Then we'll take the lift up and do a run down Boomerang to warm up. In the afternoon we can check out Hoot Brown Terrain Park . . . if you're feeling brave enough, that is." I smiled. I loved hearing Dad use all the Telluride lingo.

"I just need to drop off a bunch of Snurfer flyers and registration forms at the Village shops."

"Dad?" I asked. "Do you think I could wear Scott's old jacket this year? I've grown a little, so maybe it won't be too big for me . . ." Scott's old coat was bright yellow, super warm, and awesomely cool. It would be perfect for the Snurfer.

"Sure, but you know you can get a new jacket from the store if you want." That part of having a dad that owned a sports store was pretty cool—free gear.

"That's okay," I told Dad. "Scott's coat's already been broken in. You know, more comfortable and stuff."

"Of course," Dad answered with a wink. He knew that what you wore on the slopes wasn't all about being new and high-tech. Dad's ski-suit was legendary. He'd worn the same thing since before I was even born. It was a 1980s fluorescent blue one-piece covered with geometric shapes and patches—souvenirs from Dad's big races and events. Even though he could get any kind of new equipment he wanted, he refused. "Why would I? This still fits me perfectly! Remember, it's not what you wear, it's how you tear!" The only thing he always updated was his hat. Every year he got a new Snurfman hat, crazier than the one before.

After breakfast I walked Marty around the block. He definitely didn't have any problem with friend-making. Marty barked hello to just about every dog we passed. He sat, rolled, played dead, and tried to perform every trick in his book. "Too bad dogs can't snowboard. I bet you'd be a natural! You have to stay home today though, Marty. But don't worry. Just wait for me by the window and I'll be back before you know it."

Marty made his eyes so sad that I had to laugh. I wished he could come, but I knew the mountains were no place for pups. As I waved good-bye to Marty later that morning, I pictured him on a doggy snowboard wearing a tiny helmet. Maybe someday . . .

As we drove down Main Street I was getting more and more excited. I couldn't wait to hit the slopes. "I just need to make one quick stop at the store," said Dad.

"Aw, man! Can we hurry?" I urged.

Dad laughed. "Once you see why we're stopping at ATS, I think you'll be glad we did."

I followed Dad into the store and toward the back room. He unlocked the door to his office and there, resting on his desk, was a brand new, bright red snowboard. The letters ATS were stenciled on the top in white, lined with black. "This is for you, Ave. Only had a few made. It's the official ATS board, reserved for sponsorship of only the best young athletes."

Dad placed the board in my hands and I felt my spine shiver a little. "Whoa . . . Thanks, Dad," I said breathlessly. "This is the best present EVER!"

I got in position on the board with my legs so far apart it looked more like I was about to ride an elephant than a snowboard. Dad frowned. "I'm going to have Ricky adjust those bindings for you," he decided.

"That's probably a good idea," I laughed. I tried to fake an **ollie**, one of my favorite boarding tricks, but I felt like a Sumo wrestler with my feet spread so wide on the board. Dad called Ricky over. A guy about Tim's age with shaggy blond hair leaned over the counter.

"Can you move these in?" I showed Ricky where I wanted my bindings. "They're a little too big."

Ricky chuckled. "You can say that again. So, are you a **grommet**?" he asked. I felt my cheeks grow hot. Ricky thought I was a *beginner* at snowboarding?! I tried not to look insulted. Just because I was small didn't mean I was a grommet! "'Cause ATS is a great place to start," Ricky added. "Mr. M sells the best boards in town."

Now Dad was the one to chuckle. "Ricky, this is my daughter, Avery. She lives in Boston. And . . . she's been boarding for years. Avery's twelve."

Ricky scratched his messy hair. "Oh, sorry, Mr. M. I didn't know you guys were related. I mean . . . um . . ."

I was adopted from Korea, so obviously I looked different than the rest of my family. People who didn't know the Maddens sometimes didn't get that I was the daughter. I was pretty much used to it, but still, I never really knew what to say.

Dad helped out. "That's okay, Ricky. Avery's going to enter the Snurfer Competition on Tuesday. She's got a great chance of placing, too."

"Sweet, dude. Slap me five." Ricky bent down, held out his hand, and I gave him a good old Avery slap.

"Need anything else, Mr. M?" Ricky asked.

"Nope, we should be all set. Unless . . ." Dad looked at me with a twinkle in his eye.

"Unless what?" I asked. He didn't say anything. "Come on, Dad . . . just tell me."

"How are you for a helmet?"

I thought of my scratched-up black helmet. It had been feeling pretty tight around my ears lately. "I'd LOVE a new helmet!" I blurted.

Dad laughed. "I think that can be arranged."

"Hey, Mr. M, we just got in a whole new order of pink helmets yesterday if Avery wants to try one of those," Ricky suggested.

I looked at Dad. He looked at me. We were both thinking the same thing: NO WAY!

"That's okay, Ricky. I've already set one aside for her at the register."

"Yeah, and also . . . I really don't like pink," I explained. *That* was the understatement of the year.

I slipped on the helmet Dad had chosen—cherry red—and checked it out in the mirror. The outfit was definitely worthy of a Snurfer trophy. *But was Avery Madden worthy*?

"Need anything else?" Dad pointed to the racks of pants and tops. "Anything at all?" He held up a ski hat that looked like a Viking helmet made of fleece with two horns and long yellow yarn pigtails sewn in.

"Okay, Dad, that's just plain scary. And besides, like you say—it's not what you wear, it's how you tear . . . *it up!*" Dad laughed at my personalized version of his rule. "Now can we get outta here already? I *need* to get to the mountain!"

"No problem. I'm out of here, Ricky," Dad said. "Andie should be in shortly." And finally, we headed for the Snurfmobile. It was hard to find room for my board in the trunk. "Dad, what's your snowmobile doing back here? It's taking up all the space."

"Oh, that. I thought I'd use it later to hang a few posters for the Snurfer around town."

I rolled my eyes. My brothers and I joked that Dad

looked for any excuse to drive that thing around Telluride. Dad called it his favorite toy. I wedged my new board next to the snowmobile and we were off . . . ready to hit the slopes.

The first thing I did when we got to the mountain was sign up for the Snurfer. I filled out all my info, printing my name as neatly as I could, and dropped it into the box by the ticket window. Dad pulled out his digital camera. "Just one. We need documentation!" I got close to Dad and he held the camera in front of us with one of his long arms. "Fleas!" we cried at the same time. Dad liked "fleas" better than "cheese" because he said it made people smile more sincerely.

"There. Now we can always remember how I got my big break!" I laughed.

Dad smiled. "So should we start on Boomerang?" he asked. Boomerang was a **blue square** run, which meant that it wasn't too difficult. I knew he was choosing a blue square run for my sake—as a warm up. But it was a deep pow-pow day, so starting on a blue square was fine by me. "Oh, and here's your lift ticket."

"Thanks!" I fastened the tag on my zipper. "Are you shreddy?" I asked, pulling my goggles over my eyes.

"Are you?" Dad smiled and looked toward the mountain. "Race you to the gondola!" he declared. And with that, he took off. People turned to watch Dad pump his way through the crowd, creating a flurry of snow. He was tall and skinny in his bright blue outfit with the Snurfman jester cap flopping everywhere. It was a pretty funny sight.

"No fair, I wasn't shreddy yet!" I huffed and puffed

after him. I wasn't totally used to the altitude, either.

The gondola was free so people could ride from the base up to the Mountain Village to shop, eat, watch a competition, or just check out the view. It was going to be an amazing snowboarding day—I could tell just from looking out of the gondola. The trees were covered with snow, which meant one thing: deep powder runs.

The lift zipped us up to the top of the mountain, where fresh snow was just beginning to fall. It was finally time to ride. "Sweet runs, here I come!" I shouted as I paddled myself to a bench to buckle my boots. I was totally ready to go, but Dad was still wiping his goggles. Time for revenge. "Hey Dad . . . race you to the halfway point!" And I was off. He seemed surprised to see me float by, but smiled and waved me along. For the first ride of the season, Dad always had my back.

The trail started off slowly and I took wide, graceful turns in the fluffy snow. My legs were jelly at first, but soon I felt as if I'd never been away from the mountain. I thought of a bumper sticker on the Snurfmobile: "Born to Ride." *That's me*! I thought.

Wind whistled past my helmet and gigantic snowflakes ricocheted off my goggles. I was about to shout when I heard a loud "Whooooo-hooooo!" whizzing by. It was Dad! I went into a **tuck** position and whooshed even faster. Dad and I weaved around the trail and stopped when we reached a post with signs and arrows that told us which trails were for beginners, intermediates, experts, and the completely insane!

"Is this nirvana or what?!" Dad exclaimed.

"Ner—what?" I asked as I tried to catch my breath.

Dad laughed. "It means a state of heavenly tranquility," he explained.

"Oh yeah, then this is *definitely* nirvana!"

"Better than soccer?" Dad challenged me with a grin.

"Don't even go there! That's like . . . that's like asking me which BSG is my favorite. *Impossible*."

I was about to push off again, when Dad caught my shoulder. "Hold up a second, Ave. See that group of boarders coming down the **double black diamond**? Keep your eyes peeled for the pink helmet. Watch."

I squinted and focused in on a bright pink figure bouncing over moguls. She turned at the bottom where her trail intersected with ours and coasted toward us at avalanche speed. Just when I thought she was going to crash into me, she slid to a quick stop, sending a mini snowstorm all over us. It was a move that I used to pull on my brothers all the time . . . but no one had ever sprayed *me* with snow before!

"Jake the Snake!" said the girl. She wore a magenta jacket with orange pants. Blond braids woven with purple ribbons hung from her matching pink helmet. I had a pretty good guess where the helmet came from. The crew of boarders hung back a few yards away.

Dad held up his glove and slapped her hands in a series of high fives, like a secret handshake or something. "You almost gave me a heart attack!" Dad laughed. "Way to make an entrance!"

"How sweeeet is this shredding, Snurfman?" Pink girl pulled up her goggles. "Talk about perfect pow-pow!"

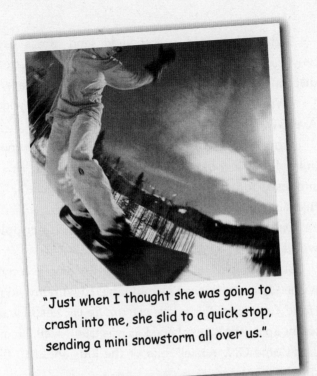

"Just when I thought she was going to crash into me, she slid to a quick stop, sending a mini snowstorm all over us."

"Better believe it!" Dad agreed and placed a hand on my shoulder. "Kazie, this is my daughter, Avery. She just got in yesterday from Boston. Avery, this is the one and only Crazie Kazie, Andie's daughter."

"Hey, nice to meet you," I said slowly.

"Nice to meet you too." Kazie grabbed my hand and squeezed—hard. She was more than a whole head taller than me, probably as tall as my friend Katani. The kids behind her all looked a little older than me too. *Were they high schoolers?* I wondered. Kazie tilted her head at them and raised her eyebrows. "You guys want to come with?" she asked.

I glanced at Dad and tried to send him a psychic message. *Say no . . . Say no . . .* But I think we must have been disconnected, because a huge grin spread on his face.

"Wow! That's nice of you, Kazie. What do you say, Ave? Want to go?"

"Um . . ." I stalled. These kids seemed cool enough, but I didn't feel like dealing with new people. This was supposed to be my day with Dad . . . not Kazie's. "Nah, that's okay," I mumbled.

Dad looked confused. "You sure? Kazie's **crippler** is world famous."

Boy, our psychic line was *way* off. For a second, I wished I were a skier so I could tap Dad with my ski pole. *Hello? Get a clue! This is kind of weird for me.* "I still want to warm up a little," I explained. It was true—well, kind of.

"Come ON, Kazie!" one of the kids shouted. "Let's shred it up already!"

"Yo, chillax," Kazie called back. "Okay, well, I'll see you tonight, Jake-the-snake-Snurf-dude-man! **Sick** riding, Avery. Later gators!" Kazie and another kid rode toward a major snow ramp and flew off it at the same time. In mid-air, they bent their knees and their snowboard bottoms smacked, **bonking** perfectly. The echo boomed through the trees even after they disappeared over the slope.

Was that my competition?

"How old is she again?" I asked.

"Thirteen."

My jaw dropped.

"She's really tall for her age," Dad added.

Now I felt more charged than ever. As we boarded

on down the mountain, I focused on my moves. No more kids' stuff. Dad and I reached the bottom and we took the chairlift back up.

"Are Kazie's parents divorced too?" I asked when we were seated in the rocking car.

"Actually, Kazie's dad died in a car accident when she was three."

"Oh," I said. I suddenly felt really sorry for Kazie. "You know my friend Charlotte? Her mom died when she was little too." I leaned against Dad, and he put his arm around me. Even though I didn't say anything, I knew he understood that I felt really lucky to have both my parents, even if I couldn't see them at the same time.

"Andie's a fantastic mom, though. She's raised Kazie all on her own and works full-time. She's helped friends open sporting goods stores in seven different states—even in New Hampshire, where Andie's from. Andie says she's a ski bum for life, but she's really talented at what she does. You know, skiing and working. And being a mom."

Dad sure did have a lot of nice things to say about Andie. I couldn't help feeling bad for my mom a little. I mean, Dad and Mom were friends and all, but still . . . "Is that why Kazie's so good at boarding?" I asked. "Getting to go all the time?"

"Well . . . it certainly doesn't hurt. You only ride a few weeks a year, and you're *still* an awesome boarder. That says something, Avery." We passed the sign that said "Ski Tips UP" and I flipped up the safety bar on the chair. Dad pulled on his goggles. "Shreddy Freddy?"

I smiled. "You bet!"

The **halfpipe** looked like, well, half of a pipe—prime for tricks and turns. The snow had been groomed carefully into two steep sides with a rounded center. I watched Dad sail down the pipe riding **fakie**, zip up the other side, catch big air, turn, and slide down. He looked up at me from the bottom.

This was it—no hesitation. I closed my eyes, took a deep breath, and cried "GERONIMO!" at the top of my lungs. My heart pounded so hard it felt like it could burst out of my chest. I went right up the side of the pipe, picking up speed till I popped into the air—really flying. I grabbed the **nose** of my board, getting perfect **slob air**, and gravity pulled me back to the icy wall. I switched my stance and slid downhill riding backward, then popped up in the air from the other side. I landed again without turning— BAM—an **air-to-fakie**. Avery Madden, Snowboarding Superstar, was BACK!

The rest of the way down the pipe was easy. I flew up the wall, made a clean **alley-oop**, rotating 180 degrees, and slid back down.

I sailed through the bottom of the pipe with both arms in the air. When I stopped, I heard a voice behind me say, "That's my girl. You've always been a natural." Dad had been watching me the whole time. I felt a warm glow inside that got bigger and bigger and spread through my entire body. "Time for a hot chocolate break?" he asked.

"Big time!" I looked up at Dad in his funny hat. This "quality time" thing was turning out to be super fun after all. "By the way, Dad, my new board is wicked cool!"

He grinned. "Ahh, *wicked*, huh?" Wicked was one

of my best funny Boston words, and Dad hadn't been to Boston in a long time.

We unsnapped our boards and headed to the Village. We could definitely handle an early lunch.

6

Eggplant

It was late afternoon by the time Dad and I got back from the slopes. I could see Marty's tail wagging from his window seat when we pulled in the driveway. I opened the door and ran inside with my boots still on. "Marty . . . I'm hoooooome!" I called.

Marty leaped into my arms and licked my face.

"Looks like the Abominable Snow Monster paid us a visit today," Dad said.

I turned and saw the trail of white chunks that my boots had left on the wooden floor. "Ooops! Can't take 'em off though! I still gotta walk Marty."

I knew that Marty was full of saved-up energy. He ran so fast around the block that we had to go around again. On round two, I demonstrated some of my halfpipe moves on little snow mounds along the sidewalk. "What do you think about this one, huh Marty man?" I slid off the pile backward and grabbed my feet. "That's called a **grab**. It looks a lot cooler on a board."

Marty spun around twice on the ground to show me he had been working on his moves too. "Not bad . . . not bad at all!" I told him. Maybe the dog-on-snowboard thing could work out after all.

When we returned home, the air was full of delicious dinner scents. "Savory," as Scott would say—the word he used to describe things that were tasty from *flavor* instead of *sweetness*.

"How did you make it smell so awesome in such a short time, Dad?"

"Funny you should ask. Actually, I keep twelve tiny cooks in the basement."

I rolled my eyes. "Dad joke alert!" I warned.

"Okay, okay. I grabbed a frozen eggplant lasagna from the freezer. Made it myself a few days ago."

While Dad cooked, I ran upstairs to take a shower. I'd just gotten back to the kitchen when the doorbell rang.

"I'll get it!" I called. I started down the hallway. Halfway there, the door burst open, sending in a gust of cold air and snow.

"Yoo-hoo, Jake, it's us." Andie poked her head around the door. She looked different from when I met her at the store. Her hair was really long and curly and her eyelashes looked longer and darker too. "Hey there, Avery!" Andie gave me a hug and kissed me on the cheek. Um . . . did she know you weren't supposed to hug *strangers*? Andie walked past me and into the kitchen, carrying a plate covered with foil.

Kazie stood frozen in the doorway for a second. She was carrying something too . . . something furry. "Like kitties?" she asked with a half smile. I stared at the large black-and-gray-striped creature twisting in her arms. That was no kitten. It was, without a doubt, the biggest cat I'd ever seen. "Meet Farkle," Kazie announced.

Farkle snarled at me, looking googley-eyed and loony. It took me a second to realize why. His eyes were two different colors! The left one was blue and the right one was gold. One of his ears stuck up and the other was squished down on his head. Farkle made a screeching *meow* when Kazie placed him on the floor. He stretched out his giant paws with SIX toes on each! Whoa. This was one spooky cat.

"He's part Maine Coon," Kazie told me proudly. "Some of 'em have extra toes."

"He's ginormous!" I reached out to pet him, but Farkle pulled his head away and made the weirdest sound ever.

"ROOOOOOOW, YEOOOOOOW."

Kazie laughed. "I wouldn't get too close if I were you. Farkle really only likes me."

I wondered what Farkle thought about other pets. "Um, I have a dog," I said. "But Marty's super people-friendly."

Kazie looked horrified. "You have a *dog*?"

"Yeah, he's the man. You want to meet him?"

"Yo, Avery, just so you know, this could be really bad news . . ." Kazie warned, but I pretended not to hear her. Marty loved kids and he'd never been afraid of cats before.

"Marty!" I called. Marty trotted into the room to see what was happening. "Hey there, lil' guy. This is Kazie and Farkle. Say hello!" I expected Marty to stand on his hind legs—his usual showoff trick, but Marty didn't move. Instead, Farkle was the one to slink closer, glaring at Marty with those freaky-deaky, multicolored eyes. Marty backed up. The hair on his back stood straight up. So did his ears and tail. Even his little legs were trembling!

Farkle the Franken-cat made the same horrible noise. *"Rooooooow, yeoooooow."*

"I stared at the large black-and-gray-striped creature twisting in her arms. That was no kitten."

That did it. Marty bounded off in the other direction, scrambled into the family room, and crawled underneath the sofa. My mouth hung open. Marty . . . a scaredy-cat? *What was wrong with this picture?!*

Kazie's mouth curled a little. It wasn't a smile . . . but not quite a frown either. She totally thought this was funny. "Told you," she said with a shrug. Farkle suddenly raced into the kitchen, and Kazie followed him.

Andie just groaned as Farkle skidded to a stop inside the kitchen doorway. "Honestly, Kazie. When are you going to let me call in an animal tamer for Farkle?" She turned to me. "I don't get what she sees in that cat. Personally, it gives me the heebie-jeebies!" *Maybe Andie isn't so bad after all*, I thought.

Kazie looked annoyed. "Farkle's a *he*, not an *it*, Mom. And he's actually really sweet. You just don't know how to handle him."

Dad walked over with a tray of drinks, ignoring the possible dog-cat war. "Who wants a root beer float? I know *someone* in here does!"

Kazie squealed. "Sweet, dude! Jake the Snake, you remembered my fave!" She grabbed one of the glasses filled with ice cream and root beer.

"Here you go, Ave." Dad held the tray in front of me.

"No thanks, Dad. You know I don't really like soda."

Dad glanced at Andie. "Still? I thought . . ."

"You don't like soda?" Kazie interrupted. "Who doesn't like soda?"

I shrugged. "I dunno. Soda just tastes funny to me." I walked over to the fridge, grabbed a bottle of spring water, and took a big swig.

"Avery's a really healthy eater, right Ave?" Dad explained. "That's why I made vegetarian lasagna."

"Whoa, whoa, whoa, hold the phone. You don't like

meat, either?" Kazie stared at me like I was from another planet or something.

"I like some meat. I eat turkey wraps all the time," I told Kazie. "Just not usually steak. I mean of course I like Fat Alley burgers—"

"OMG, I live on them!" Kazie took a long slurp of her float. "How could you *not like* meat?" she repeated.

"I said—" I began, but Dad interrupted.

"Ladies and . . . well . . . ladies. Dinner is served," he announced. He looked so proud of himself that Kazie, Andie, and I all cracked up.

"Yes, master chef. *Merci!*" Andie replied.

Sitting down to dinner at the table in the family room was a relief. Everyone filled their plates and dug in.

"This is off-the-hook delish, Snurfman . . . way better than Mom's," Kazie said with her mouth full of eggplant.

"Hey!" Andie warned playfully.

"Dad's an awesome cook," I told them. "So is my big brother Scott. He's actually at culinary school right now. . . . Or else he'd be here now. My mom's definitely more of a takeout type."

"Mine too," agreed Kazie.

Andie blushed. "I hear you're a quite a good boarder, Avery," she said, probably wanting to change the subject. "Are you going to enter the competition?"

"Already did!" I exclaimed.

Kazie took a bite of garlic bread and licked the butter off her fingers. "Right on. Snurfer Competition, *hollaaa*! I'm going for number one. Check out my Donnie Keeler impression." She jumped up and did a **ho-ho**, planting both hands on her pretend snowboard.

"Not during dinner, Kazie!" Andie shook her head and sighed. "I've never had that much energy in my entire life. I don't know where she gets it."

I didn't know either. And also, if Kazie was in the same division as me, I didn't know if I had a prayer at the Snurfer. At least not after what I'd seen today.

"Don't move," Andie said when everyone had finished the main course. "I brought dessert."

Andie ran to the kitchen and returned with the large foil-covered platter. She put down the plate and took off the foil. Dessert was . . . cheese?

"Here ve go. Ze plate of ze fabulouso cheeses of ze vorld!" Andie declared in a funny fake accent.

Kazie didn't look happy though. "Party foul, Mom!" she groaned. "I thought you were bringing *cheesecake* . . . not *cheese*. This is soooo not a dessert. Right, Avery?"

"Um . . . um . . ." I stuttered. I had to admit though, I agreed with Kazie. Cheese for dessert? No way.

"I didn't have time for cheesecake, Kazie," Andie explained, even though she was looking at Dad. "Besides, you like cheese. Don't you like cheese, Avery?"

I looked at the plate full of strange, colorful cheeses. "Only on sandwiches and pizza," I answered. Hey, I couldn't lie to her.

"Ha! See, Mom. Told you."

"I bet I can solve this problem." Dad dug in his pocket and pulled out some bills. "Why don't you girls walk down to The Sweet Life and get some ice cream?" Dad handed the money to Kazie.

I swallowed. I knew Kazie was sitting closer to Dad, but still . . . couldn't he just split the money and give us each enough to pay for ourselves? I mean, just because Kazie was a year older than me, it didn't mean she was my *babysitter*.

"I'm going to take Marty along for the walk. He's not usually this shy." I got up to find Marty, who was still cowering under the big red couch. Sitting on top of the cushion, like a king on his throne, was Franken-Farkle, washing his giant mutant paws with his tongue. He took one look at me and hissed.

Kazie walked in and started to laugh. "Farkle, Farkle, bad kitty. Did Wittle Farkle Warkle scare Marty?"

"Marty's not scared," I defended him, quickly adding, "he's just not used to the Colorado weather. He's probably cold, and it's warm under there, near the heating vent. Yeah. He's cold is all."

"Doesn't it get cold in Boston?" Kazie smiled at me. "Come on, leave him here. I'm leaving Farkle."

Kazie left the room and snapped open her cell phone. I looked under the sofa and sighed. I really didn't want to leave Marty with Farkle, the demented feline from the Black Lagoon. But I knew that there was no way I'd be able to coax him out from his hiding place. At least not with "Wittle Farkle Warkle" around.

Kazie came back in the room. "Great news. I just called my friends and they're going to meet us at The Sweet Life."

"You called your friends?" *Be quiet, Avery!* I told myself. I sounded like an echo. But I wasn't sure I wanted to hang out at The Sweet Life with Kazie, much less all of her friends.

"Sure. They're way cool. You'll love 'em." Kazie grabbed her coat, and headed for the door. "Come on, Avery. Let's go."

7

Mute Air

"Cool headband," Kazie said as she and I walked toward town.

"Headband?" I reached up and felt my Kgirl ear warmer. "Oh, yeah. Thanks. My friend Katani made it for me especially for this trip."

"Nice. Hey, I bet we could sell those at ATS. I know how to put in orders of like, any model. You see my helmet today? That was all me. A KZ original!" Whoa, was this girl taking over my life?

"Well I don't think my friend would like it if I just copied her design and sold it. This, um, headband is a Kgirl original."

"Kgirl original?" Kazie laughed. "Sounds like *she* copied *me* already."

I was about to point out that Katani didn't even know her, but suddenly a kid shouted from across the street. "Yo, Crazie Kaz!"

"Hey, Jimbo!" Kazie waved, then turned to me and

explained, "He's part of my crew. What was I saying? Oh, yeah. Jake lets me design all sorts of stuff for ATS. It's sooo easy. I just look through the catalog and choose the color and pattern. Like the snowboard I made for the Snurfer Competition. It's totally off the hook! Okay, ready?" Kazie jumped in front of me and spread her arms out in front of my face like there was a big invisible snowboard there. "Bright red, freestyle shape with the letters ATS on the front and back. It's the official ATS board for the season. How sick is that going to be to race on?" Kazie slipped ahead and pretended to board along the sidewalk.

I felt kind of dizzy. My new snowboard was a KZ original? Dad hadn't ever let *me* make designs for him before. Not that I was into that kind of thing, stick figures being my best artwork. But still, he hadn't even asked me! Since when did he let kids make ATS snowboards? And why did he think I'd *want* a KZ original anyway? Suddenly I got a funny feeling in my stomach.

"My dad gave me one of those ATS boards, actually," I said carefully to Kazie. "It's a *pretty* good ride." It was better than a pretty good ride. It was downright awesome. But that was the board . . . NOT Kazie's so-called "design." "So I guess we'll be racing on the same board then," I went on, quickly, trying to stay cool. "Hope we don't get them confused, right?" I knew I should be polite, but I felt like my mouth was just running out of control. It always did that when I was starting to get angry.

Kazie slid across a frozen puddle. "No way, man," she laughed, "I'm **goofy-footed**. My bindings are on the opposite side as yours." Maybe that's why they called her

Crazie Kazie. Goofy-footed Kazie was a right-foot-forward girl. "Plus your bindings are closer together than mine. So don't worry—we'll never get mixed up."

"Shred Betty!" someone called from a car passing by. "Nice moves today!"

Geesh, how many names does this girl have? I wondered.

Kazie gave the car a double thumbs-up and kept fake boarding down the sidewalk.

"I guess everyone knows you in Telluride." I hoped I didn't sound jealous.

"That's nothing. Coaches come to the mountain all the time to watch me. It can be annoying . . . like I always have to be trying my best, you know?"

"You're lucky!" I said. "I'd love it if coaches came to watch me board. But I only see my dad for a little bit in the winter so . . ."

"You're the one who's lucky. Jake's a sick boarder. I bet it's way awesome to have him as a dad." Kazie's voice was quieter than usual. She stopped sliding around and looked at me.

"It is," I replied. "My dad—"

But she quickly interrupted. "*My* dad was an awesome skier though." She went back to practicing.

"Yeah?"

"Totally. He could have gone to the Olympics. Would have, I mean."

"Wow," I murmured. Hanging out with Kazie was sort of stressful compared to the BSG. I never knew the right thing, or the cool thing, to say, but here I was feeling . . . well . . . bad for her. "Do you miss him?" I asked.

"Sometimes," Kazie said quietly. Then she jumped on a snow bank and got loud again. "But whatever. I've got plenty of people in my life . . . believe me."

Plenty of people? Did she not miss her dad anymore because now she had MY DAD? I suddenly had a thought. If Andie and Dad got married, then Kazie would be my sister . . . or stepsister. Whoa. *Wait till I tell the BSG about this one.* I had a sudden image of a Farkle/Marty war in the bathroom.

"Kazie! There you are!" called a girl as tall as Kazie with long red hair. She popped out from a video store in front of us with another shorter, blonde friend.

"Crazieeeee!" the blonde one hollered.

"Hey girls! What's crack-a-lackin'?" Kazie said.

"How was your dinner with the new girl?" asked the red-headed one.

"Yeah! What's the Snurfman's daughter like?" asked the other.

Helloooo! Was I invisible? Time to take matters into my own hands. "Hey guys! I'm Avery." They stared at me blankly. "The Snurfman's daughter . . ." I clarified.

"Oh, yeah. Avery, these are my friends, Siobhan and Tessa," Kazie said.

"You're the Snurfman's daughter?" asked Tessa, the girl with red hair.

"Yup."

Siobhan looked me up and down. "How old are you?"

"Twelve. How old are you?"

"Thirteen," they said at the same time.

"Well, do you race?" Siobhan asked. By looking at Siobhan I could tell that she did. Her style was like something out of a snowboarding magazine. Her streaked blonde hair was super short and all spiky. *Like Farkle,* I thought.

"Yeah, I race. I'm gonna be in the Snurfer," I told them.

The girls started to giggle. "That's not what she means," Kazie said. She looked at the two girls and winked. "Last one to The Sweet Life is a rotten eggplant!"

Before I knew what was happening, the three of them took off sprinting. But so did I. Running was one of my specialties. Even though Kazie and her friends had a head start, I passed them all in seconds and didn't look back.

I got to The Sweet Life and collapsed onto the front step. "Winner!" I cried and looked around for the girls. Siobhan and Tessa were a block behind and not going all that fast. Kazie was even farther. They jogged over to me at a mellow pace . . . not even out of breath.

"Winner!" I cried again and put my hand out for them to slap.

The girls were laughing hysterically. "Congratulations, Avery. You're officially the ice cream cleaner-upper for the night," Tessa proclaimed.

My throat felt dry. Since when did winning a race make you the loser? I glared at Kazie, who shrugged. "Chill, Avery. It's just a joke. Consider it . . . your initiation."

Tessa, Siobhan, and Kazie, still laughing, tumbled into the store.

Was this what it was like to be the new kid in Telluride? Definitely not what we did to Charlotte and Isabel when they were new to Brookline. Who did this Kazie girl think she was?

"Last one to The Sweet Life is a rotten eggplant!"

8

Melon

When I walked down the stairs into The Sweet Life I could feel everybody staring at me. Good thing I wasn't a blusher like Charlotte or my face would be big-time red. Kazie, Tessa, and Siobhan were already in line at the counter. Everyone was trying to talk to Crazie Kazie. Boy, was she popular in Telluride—it didn't take me long to figure that one out.

Kazie got her ice cream—a banana split—and turned to find a table. Then I couldn't believe my eyes. The huge crowd of kids in the store parted just so Kazie could have a path to walk through. Tessa and Siobhan followed. A few younger girls sitting at the big corner booth scrambled to get up, and Kazie and her friends settled right into their places. I'd never seen anything like this, except in movies.

"Yo, Avery!" Kazie shouted. "You coming?"

I squeezed through the crowd (no one moved out of the way for *me*) and went over to their booth, which was now totally filled with people. "I need the money," I said.

Kazie cupped her ear. "I can't hear you. Everybody be quiet!" she commanded.

All the kids instantly stopped talking.

"I need the money," I repeated. Now everyone was listening. I was suddenly really mad at Dad for giving Kazie the money to hold.

"Oh, yeah!" Kazie reached into her pocket and scrunched some bills into my hand. "I totally forgot. Soooorry. Here it is."

"Don't sweat it," I mumbled and turned to go back. I wished Kazie wouldn't make such a big scene over everything. She seemed all laid-back, but it looked to me like underneath it all she was really a total drama queen.

"Do you even eat ice cream?" Kazie called with a smug laugh. I didn't answer, but I could hear her quietly telling her friends about what happened with the root beer floats.

"Can I help you?" asked the boy behind the counter.

"Do you still have fruit smoothies?" I asked him. (It just so happens I did eat ice cream. But fruit smoothies were definitely my fave.)

"You bet." The boy smiled and pointed to a sign that listed smoothie flavors. "What kind?"

There were so many yummy fruits to choose from, how could I decide? "Hmm . . . eenie, meanie, miney, pineapple! No, mango . . . no, melon . . . no—"

"How 'bout all three?"

"Excellent!"

I got my smoothie and went back to the table. It was completely packed. Did every kid in Telluride want to hang out with the great Crazie Kazie? What was so great about her, anyway? Kazie was telling a story about the time her board unhooked on the middle of a chairlift and she had to shimmy up a double black diamond to get it back. "Wanna hear the best part? One of my boots went down with it!"

"That's sick!" a boy exclaimed.

"Let's put it this way—they don't call her Crazie Kazie for nothing!" said Tessa.

"You guys think *that*'s crazy," I began. "Two years ago I got stuck on this trail that was blocked off because of an avalanche warning. I had to find my way through the woods in the middle of a monster blizzard . . . and I wasn't even **glading**!"

The crowd got quiet again and suddenly all eyes were on me. I was the center of attention now, and for some reason it didn't feel too cool.

"Who are you?" asked the girl beside me.

"I'm Avery. Avery Madden."

"Why does that name sound familiar?" asked someone else.

"Her dad's Jake Madden . . . aka the Snurfman . . . aka MY BOSS!" Kazie explained.

Everyone nodded and "ohhed." *Aka your mom's boyfriend*, I thought.

I was about to explain that although I usually lived in Boston, I wasn't really a new kid at all . . . when the bell over the door jingled. Everyone looked to see who was coming down the stairs.

It was a boy about my age. He was tall, taller than Kazie

even, with dark curly hair and bright red cheeks, probably from being outside. The girls around me were all staring and whispering . . . including Kazie, Tessa, and Siobhan. I'd been friends with Maeve long enough to know what *those* kind of looks meant. This kid—whoever he was—must've been THE cute boy of Telluride. I guess every town had one.

I thought he'd probably go right over the table and join the Crazie Kazie Fan Club, but he didn't. *Weird*, I thought. Then I saw something really weird. The front of the kid's jacket was *moving*. "Whoa!" he cried suddenly. I couldn't believe my eyes. A ferret popped out of his collar, leaped onto his shoulder, and then crawled to his head.

"Check it out! Jason brought his ferret. Hey, Jason, come here!" Kazie called. "Can I pet him?"

Jason slowly reached up to snatch the ferret off his head. Just as his hand was about to clamp down on the furry dude, the ferret scrambled back onto Jason's shoulder and took a flying leap onto a nearby table before disappearing underneath it. Jason groaned. "Radley, no!" he exclaimed, kneeling under the table and looking around for the escapee.

The store manager hurried toward Jason shaking a finger. "What did I tell you about bringing that rodent in here? Health regulations strictly prohibit animals!" That *really* made my blood boil. *Ferrets weren't rodents.* Seriously. It says so in the encyclopedia. Suddenly a table of girls across the room screamed, and Jason's face turned even redder than before. "Come on, kid! Now find that rodent and get it outta here," the manager growled.

"Yes sir. I'll do that." *How* he was going to do that was

the question. Jason looked terrified as he stood up and surveyed the room, but actually the screams were good news—now we knew where the ferret was. I decided to use a little Avery Animal Mastermind.

"Okay, everybody, stay calm!" I instructed. Jason looked confused. "Don't worry," I told him. "I've done this thousands of times before." Okay, that was a lie. I had done it once before. And it hadn't been a ferret so much as a guinea pig. And it wasn't so much my guinea pig—it was Maeve's . . . the time I was baby-sitting for it. And I didn't actually *catch* the guinea pig. But hey, close enough, right?

I put my smoothie on the table by Kazie and tried to spot the long, furry animal.

"Radley, Radley, come back here," Jason called. Everyone was giggling a little, except for the group of girls who were shrieking with their legs curled up on the benches. People could be so silly—ferrets were totally safe and cute. Poor Jason though. He looked way embarrassed. Good thing I was on the case.

I heard a clinking sound by the radiator, and I quickly grabbed half a banana from Kazie's sundae. "I'm going to have to borrow this," I said. Ferrets went nuts for bananas.

"Hey!" Kazie cried.

"Do you want me to catch the ferret or not?" I asked.

That made her quiet. She flipped her long blonde hair over her shoulder and went "Hmph!"

I got down on my hands and knees, scooted under the table, and wiggled the banana near a tiny crack under the radiator. "Here, Radley, want a snack?" I made my voice very soft and soothing. Talking to animals was a specialty of mine. "You know you're hungry, little guy. You want a bite?" I waved the banana then pulled it back again.

"Look! It's working!" shouted one of the kids.

Radley's nose twitched as he inched toward me. I kept pulling the banana back more and more until Radley was all the way out. Just as he got close enough to nibble, I reached under the radiator and grabbed. Game over! Mission accomplished! Ferret captured!

"Wow, that was awesome, Avery!" said Tessa. Actually, the whole Kazie-crew was smiling at me . . . except for Kazie. I hoped she wasn't mad that I nabbed her banana.

Just then, someone tapped me on the shoulder. I was so startled, I almost let go of Radley. It was Jason. "Thanks," he said, looking very relieved. "That was close."

"No prob. Here you go!" I slid Radley into his hands.

"How many ferrets do you have?" he asked.

I laughed. "Zero. But I do have a snake and a frog, and a dog that I share with my friends."

"So then how did you . . . ?" Jason held up Radley. His face was still pink. Charlotte would laugh when I told her that guys could be wicked bad blushers too.

I shrugged. "I'm pretty good when it comes to animals."

I waited for him to say something, but Jason just stood there totally zoned out. "I shouldn't have brought Radley in here," he mumbled finally. "I gotta go." He put the ferret in his pocket and dashed out the door.

"Hey, wait a sec!" I cried. I really wanted to talk to this kid. I mean, who brings a ferret to an ice cream store in

Telluride? It was so random and very, very cool.

I started to follow him out when I felt someone grab my arm again. *Yikes.* Kazie took a giant step to position herself between me and the door. "I wouldn't, Avery," she warned. "Jason's new here and he's really shy. He probably just wants to be left alone."

"But—"

Siobhan folded her arms and stood beside Kazie. "Seriously. I've been trying all month to talk to him. Just forget it. He doesn't even like Kazie." She giggled and Kazie elbowed her in the side.

"We all know you think he's cute, Avery," Tessa added, "but just give it up."

I couldn't help but laugh at that one. "You guys, I don't think he's—"

"Come on," Kazie said. "I'm gonna tell the story about the time I took the *worst* **digger** at Deer Valley in Utah." But she didn't sit back down and ignore me like she had before. She was waiting for me to . . . to what? To go back to the table and NOT hang out with Jason? Kazie, Tessa, and Siobhan had pretty much formed a wall in front of me. Hmm . . . how to escape?

"Hey, everyone! Is that Donnie Keeler?" I pointed to a table in the back.

"Where!?" Kazie and her friends shouted at once. The second they turned, I pulled my ear warmer over my ears, slipped between Kazie and Tessa, and ran out the door.

"Catch you on the flip side!" I was off.

CHAPTER

9
Ollie

H ey, Jason, wait up!" Jason was already a few blocks ahead, so this time my sprinting came in handy.

Now Jason was the one who was startled. "Hey! Ferret-catcher girl."

"Right! Ferret catcher girl! That's me. Otherwise known as Avery. And you're Jason." He shook my hand quickly and looked at the ground. Oops . . . Kazie mentioned that he was shy. He was probably wondering why some random girl was chasing him down the street. "That ferret escape was the only funny thing that's happened all night," I explained.

To my relief, Jason laughed. "Really? I guess taking Radley in there was not my smartest idea ever. Usually he stays inside my shirt—no problem. He was going crazy tonight, though."

"He probably smelled all the delicious goodies in there! FYI, ferrets love sweet stuff, but a lot of sugary snacks are really bad for them."

"Wow," said Jason. "How do you know so much about ferrets?"

I shrugged. "I'm sort of a whiz when it comes to animal trivia. How long have you had this guy?"

"Just got him. I've had tons of pets, but this is my first ferret. I'm still getting used to Radley."

I reached out and patted Radley's wiggly little nose with my finger.

"Hey!" Jason said. "You wanna hold him?"

"Sure!"

Jason carefully handed me the ferret and I cuddled him in both hands. Then I unzipped my jacket and tucked him inside in case he was cold. I giggled when he squirmed around in there. Finally Radley curled into a ball and stayed still.

The streets of Telluride were so calm at night. Way different than with the daytime traffic. It wasn't scary-quiet, though. Just peaceful.

"So how come you call him Radley?" I asked finally. "It's a cool name."

"Short for Boo Radley. He's a character from the book *To Kill a Mockingbird*. That's my favorite book. You ever read it?"

I nodded. "Yeah, we read it earlier this year. Everyone in the seventh grade at my school has to. What grade are you in?"

"Eighth," he answered. "So I take it you aren't from around here?"

"Nope. Boston. My dad lives in Telluride though, so I'm visiting for the week."

"Boston? Whoa . . . that's so far. I've never been further east than Nebraska."

"Nebraska? What's in Nebraska?" I asked.

Jason smiled. "Not much, actually. My parents used to live there . . . in Omaha. Then I moved to Durango, Colorado, with my grandparents. And then I moved here about . . . hmm . . . I guess two months ago now."

"Do you like Telluride?"

Jason shrugged. "I dunno. It's okay, I guess. My foster family is nice, though."

Foster family? I wondered what that was all about. Jason was the second kid I'd met in two days who had a different kind of family than mine. I wanted to ask him more about it—where his real parents were, why he'd moved around so much—but I didn't know if those were the type of questions you asked a new friend. And I didn't like it when people asked me too many nosy questions.

"Do you—" We both started talking at the same time, then we burst out laughing.

"You go," I said.

"Do you like the Red Sox?" Jason asked. "They're my favorite team. My grandpa's originally from Boston, and I mean, you're from Boston, right? So I figured—"

"*Like* the Red Sox?" I interrupted. "DO I LIKE THE RED SOX?"

"Umm . . ."

"I LOVE THEM!" I cried. "Seriously! I am a Red Sox superfan. I follow every game. I'm *obsessed*." Jason stared at me with huge eyes, but I couldn't stop. Once I heard the words "Red Sox" there was no turning back. "One time, I even got to meet Robbie Flores . . . Rookie of the Year. He's probably, like, THE COOLEST player of all time."

"You met Robbie Flores?" Jason was definitely impressed—I could tell. We walked down Main Street, and I told Jason all about Marty running away and how Robbie Flores found him and thought he was good luck. I knew I was getting farther and farther from my house but I didn't really mind. It was so exciting to talk to someone from so far away who loved animals and the Red Sox, just like me. "And so the BSG—that's what me and my friends call ourselves—we got to go Fenway and meet Flores! It was sooo cool!"

"Wow," Jason said. "Did you get Marty back?"

I nodded. "Sure did. He's here with me right now. Well, back at my dad's house. If you like animals, you'll loooove Marty. Sometimes I feel like he's really a person trapped in the body of a dog. I know, I know, it sounds really weird . . . but when you meet him you'll understand." I shivered and rubbed my hand over my jacket to make sure Radley was warm enough in there.

"No, I know what you mean," said Jason. "That's how it is with Ollie."

"Who's Ollie?"

Jason smiled. He kind of reminded me of Nick Montoya. Something about the way he just did his own thing without caring too much about what other people thought. "Ollie's . . ." Jason started to explain. "Hey! You want to meet him? We're almost at my house. It's right on Townsend—the yellow one on the corner. And I don't know about you . . . but I'm freezing!" He pulled his winter hat over his ears and blew on his hands. "My foster mom makes the best hot chocolate."

I'd left my unfinished smoothie back at The Sweet Life, and something sweet like hot chocolate did sound tempting. "Totally!" I agreed. Then I remembered. "What about my dad? I don't have a cell phone with me to tell him where I am."

"You can use the phone at my house. And someone can give you a ride home for sure."

"Deal," I said. "Then tomorrow you can meet Marty!"

Jason smiled. We were right under a street lamp and with the light shining on his face, I noticed something. His eyes were really, really blue. Not regular blue like Maeve's eyes, but light. Like the sky almost. In the dark they practically glowed.

"You know . . ." I started to say as we walked up Townsend Street.

"Yeah?"

I was about to tell him that he had the coolest eyes but then I realized how girly and weird that sounded. So I blurted out the first thing that popped into my head. "Blue's my favorite color." *Good one, Avery*, I thought.

"Okay," Jason said. "Um, mine too . . ."

I bit my bottom lip and tried to think of something else to say. "Last one to your house is a rotten eggplant! I mean, egg. I mean . . . oh, whatever. Race you!"

"Huh?" Jason was so confused by the whole race thing that I had a major head start. I could have won no prob, but I slowed down a little. I had to be careful to hold Radley securely against my chest, and I wanted Jason to know that

Avery Madden was no cheater. Then just before we got to his fence, *he passed me*. No way! I picked up my speed again and caught up with him at the very last second. We were both laughing as we slapped his front door at exactly the same time.

"Hey, everybody," Jason called as we opened the door. Radley poked his head out of my jacket the minute we stepped inside. "I'm back!" His house was cozy on the inside. It was full of little snowmen decorations and some kids' pictures on the wall. There was only one of Jason though—a school picture. It must have been new.

Jason saw me checking out the photos. "They've had other kids stay here before, but right now it's only me and Frankie. Frankie's been here since he was four."

We heard footsteps getting closer and a door swung open. "Hey! I know you," said a cheerful voice. It was Bonnie from Fat Alley! She looked just as nice as always, except this time she was wearing jeans and a green fleece pullover instead of her Fat Alley uniform.

"Wow, Bonnie's your foster mom?" I turned to Jason and back to Bonnie. "Hi! I like your house."

"Thanks, Avery. Come on in. Make yourself at home. Can I get you some hot chocolate, extra marshmallows, hold the whipped cream? How about you, Jason?"

"Sure, Bonnie. Thanks!" I said. I took off my ear warmer, tucked it safely into my coat pocket, and settled into a comfy chair by the fireplace.

Bonnie pushed the door into the kitchen to go get the hot chocolate, but as she did, a little kid suddenly raced under her arm and into the room. He flew straight past

Bonnie and grabbed Jason around the legs so tightly that Jason almost fell over. Bonnie laughed and continued into the kitchen.

The kid wouldn't let go of Jason's legs. "Hi, Jason! Hi, Jason! Where's Radley? Can I hold him? Can I?"

"Hey there, buddy," Jason said. "Avery, this is my foster brother, Frankie. Frankie, this is Avery."

I recognized Frankie from the pictures on the walls. He was the one with crazy brown hair that stuck out in messy spikes all over the place and lots of freckles.

"Hi, Frankie. How old are you?" I asked, bending over.

Frankie held up two hands—five fingers on one hand and one on the other. "*Six,*" he announced proudly. I wanted to laugh at how puffed up Frankie was getting for just being six.

Jason looked at me. "Frankie just had a birthday. Tell Avery what you got," Jason suggested.

Frankie shook his head. "No, I don't wanna." Frankie's eyes never left the wiggling bundle of ferret in my jacket. "Jason, can I hold Radley now?" he pleaded.

Jason nodded. "Sure. Just be careful."

I lifted Radley out of my coat and passed him to Jason. Radley's bright eyes looked around and settled on the sight of two six-year-old hands coming closer. Frankie grasped Radley for only a second before the ferret slithered out of his hands and scampered under the couch.

"Ohh . . ." Frankie sighed. "I'm sorry."

"That's okay, buddy," Jason assured him. "Radley's right here." He reached under the couch and scooped up the ferret. "But guess who Avery and I are about to go visit?"

Frankie's eyes lit up. "Ollie!"

Jason smiled. "Yup."

Frankie jumped up and down and tugged on Jason's coat. "Jason, can I come? Can I be your assistant? I know how to. Pleeease?"

At the sound of footsteps, Jason put a finger up to his lips and said, "Shhh!" But Frankie wasn't paying attention.

He went running out of the room the moment Bonnie returned holding a tray with three mugs. "We run a zoo here, Avery, in case you hadn't noticed." She laughed as a little person in a winter coat whizzed back through the door and into the hallway. "Now just where does Frankie think he's going?"

Without missing a beat, Jason explained, "I'm going to go show Avery my birdhouses." Birdhouses, huh? Was that a lie or a clue or both?

Bonnie nodded. "Well, that's fine. But would you grab Frankie on your way? It's too late and too chilly for him to be out playing . . . I don't want him to catch a cold."

"Yo, Frankie!" Jason called. We heard the sound of little footsteps retreating. "Not tonight, buddy. You can be my assistant tomorrow," he promised, handing Frankie a fireball from his pocket. A fireball candy obviously wasn't a good enough substitute for Ollie. Frankie put his hands on his hips and frowned. "And remember," Jason whispered, "this is top secret! Let's spit on it."

Frankie thoughtfully removed the fireball from his

mouth and squeezed it in one fist while he neatly spit into the other. Then he turned and glowered at me. "Thanks a lot," he muttered and took off running through the house.

Jason handed Radley off to Bonnie. I got my coat and followed Jason out, but first asked Bonnie, "Can you save my hot chocolate for me for when we get back? Please?"

She smiled. "Of course, honey."

Then I had to run to keep up with Jason. He was like Radley . . . always slipping away. I couldn't wait to see who (or what) Ollie was. Maybe a boa constrictor. I used to want my own boa, but Mom practically had a heart attack when I mentioned the idea. Only Walter-sized snakes were allowed.

"Frankie doesn't have a lot of patience," Jason explained as we walked across the yard. "Bonnie said it's hard for him to trust new people."

I wondered what Frankie's story was, but again, I wasn't sure if that was too nosy of a question. "How'd you get him to trust you?" I asked instead.

Jason paused and thought about this as we trampled through the trees. "I dunno. I've always been good with wounded animals and stuff. Frankie sort of reminds me of one. Does that sound weird?"

I shook my head. "It makes sense to me." I did know what he meant. Kids who needed extra love and attention made me think of wounded animals too . . . scared and a little suspicious at the same time.

I followed Jason down a snowy path behind the house to a small, rundown shed. It was leaning slightly to one side, probably from the winds and the weight of all the snow on the roof. Jason unlocked the door and opened it with a *creeeak*.

Inside it was dark and smelled like rotting wood. Cobwebs stretched over the beams and tools hung on the walls. As my eyes got used to the dim light, I looked around for a cage and listened as hard as I could for some kind of animal sound. Nothing. Where was he keeping this thing? Then, from behind a cabinet, I saw something move . . . or flutter!

"Wow . . ." I breathed. "Is that what I think it is?"

Jason pulled a cord hanging from the ceiling and switched on a single light bulb. "Avery, meet Ollie," he said and walked over to a huge brown bird perched in the corner of the shed. "Ollie's a genuine, wild, red-tailed hawk." He began to walk slowly toward Ollie. "I found him on the ground in the woods. He's not fully grown yet. See, you can tell by how his irises are still kind of yellow. But he's definitely not a baby, either . . . I think he must have been injured by some other animal. Nothing was broken, but he didn't seem like he could fly on his own."

I blinked, still in shock. I'd never seen a wild bird so close-up before. "Poor little guy. It's a really good thing you found him, Jason. He never would have survived out there alone."

Jason nodded. "I know."

"But Jason . . ." I took a deep breath. "I thought people weren't allowed to keep wild creatures. In fact, I'm pretty sure it's illegal. Don't you need to contact a shelter or some kind of animal rescue group?"

Jason shook his head. "See, my grandpa was a falconer,

and he also ran a licensed hawk sanctuary in Durango. I've helped Gramps raise at least ten hawks . . . even ones that had broken wings. Seriously, I know *everything* about these guys. With babies, it's really dangerous for humans to be around them a lot, because the hawks get confused and start to think they're people instead of birds! But Ollie's old enough to know the difference. When he's ready, I'm going to release him to the wild. But for now, I have to keep him a secret."

"Are you sure?" I asked Jason, still feeling kind of funny about the situation. "When I visited Montana, my friends and I found these abandoned wolf pups and really wanted to take care of them. But my friend's dad told us we could get in BIG trouble, and he found a wildlife rescue group to help them instead."

"It's kind of risky for me to keep Ollie here, but I know that I can help him," Jason assured me.

"So how'd you convince Bonnie to let you keep him?"

Jason looked at me and admitted, "I didn't tell her."

I nodded and understood. That was what the BSG did when we first found Marty, before we found out it was okay for Charlotte to keep a dog in her house after all. I watched as Ollie noticed Jason and perked up his head. "What about Frankie?" I remembered how Frankie had asked to come out and visit Ollie when Bonnie was making hot chocolate.

"Frankie knows, but he'd never say anything. It makes him feel special to have a secret to keep."

"So what do your, um, foster parents think you're doing out here?" I couldn't help but ask.

Jason smiled. "Bonnie and Fred told me I could use the shed as my own private space for my birdhouses. See?" He pointed to a work table and cabinets behind it. The cabinets were full of these little birdhouses made from pieces of bark and other miscellaneous things Jason had collected. He had boxes and boxes of supplies, all labeled: TWINE, PEBBLES, BUTTONS, and CHINA AND GLASS. The birdhouses looked more like little homes for gnomes or fairies. Anyone who got to live in one of these was one lucky bird.

"Whoa, Jason . . . these are sooo cool! I wish I could take a picture to show my friend Isabel. She'd go crazy over them . . . birds are her favorite animals to draw."

Jason looked at the ground and scraped at the dirt with his shoe. "It's just a weird hobby. Something my grandma taught me."

"I bet you could sell these, you know," I told him.

Jason shook his head. "I'm not *that* good," he said, still looking down.

I opened my mouth to tell him that he was, but a squawk came from the dim corner where Ollie was marching around. "Hey there, Ollie." Jason slowly walked to the hawk.

"Has taking care of him been a lot of work?" I asked.

He laughed. "See that sleeping bag? I had to sneak out here to sleep for almost a week. Then I spent four hours a day sitting with him, talking to him, and trying to get him to eat by feeding him scraps of raw hamburger. I even started doing my homework out here. But it's paid off. Ollie's almost ready to be released. I'm probably going to do it this week."

Jason studied Ollie very carefully, like he was trying to figure out exactly what the hawk needed. There was something really special about Jason and Ollie, like they absolutely trusted each other one hundred percent. I'd never seen a kid my own age so comfortable around a wild creature like that. "He must really love you," I said. "I mean, since you raised him and all . . ." Did that sound silly? I glanced at Jason out of the corner of my eye, but he wasn't laughing.

"No. When Ollie flies away, he'll forget all about me and be fine on his own. Hawks aren't like dogs. Wild birds and animals need to be free. Hawks can be devoted to their trainers, but they never love you."

"But that's sad." I didn't want to believe that this hawk would forget the boy who saved his life.

"No, it's okay. That's just how hawks are," Jason insisted. "Ollie trusts me to give him food, and I trust that Ollie will stay here and not try to escape. You must be hungry, huh fella?" Jason went over to a small cage and got something out, keeping his back turned to me . . . like he didn't want me to know or see whatever it was he was giving Ollie. But I had a guess.

"Are you feeding him a mouse right now?" I asked. "Can I watch?"

Jason raised his eyebrows. "Seriously? I figured you'd be totally freaked out if you knew. Mice are Ollie's favorite."

I shrugged. "Hey, I'm a snake owner, don't forget. I've fed Walter—that's my snake—plenty of mice before. It's just a part of nature, right?"

"Right. And besides, it could be worse. Did you know that mother hawks chew up mice and other rodents and then regurgitate them into their babies' mouths?"

I made a grossed-out face. "Ugh. I'll stick to the mice-feeding, thanks."

Jason slid his right hand into a worn leather glove. "Me too. I just close the shed door and let the mouse go. Ollie always catches it. The more practice he gets flying and hunting on his own, the sooner he can go back to the wild where he belongs." He untied the leash that fastened Ollie to his perch then stepped behind me, put two hands on my shoulders, and moved me away from the cage. "Okay, Avery. Step back and watch. And whatever you do, don't open the shed door."

"What are those thingies called?" I pointed to the little leather bands around each leg above the bird's feet, both attached to what looked like a cut-up jump rope.

"Those are anklets. And the straps are called jesses. This way he can move back and forth on his perch without getting tangled, but he can't leave the perch unless I turn him loose. Check it out."

Jason stepped back and blew one sharp note on a whistle he wore around his neck. Ollie flapped twice, lifted off the perch, and landed on Jason's outstretched glove.

"He loves flying, which is a good sign," Jason explained as he smoothed Ollie's feathers.

"Me too!" I said and then realized how that sounded. "I mean, I obviously can't fly, but I feel like I am when I'm snowboarding. It's the best."

"You snowboard?"

"Are you kidding? What else would I do in Telluride? I'm going to be in the Snurfer Competition on Tuesday. I can't wait! You're doing it too, right?" I figured someone who named his hawk "Ollie" would definitely be a snowboarding nut like me.

But Jason shook his head. "Um, no. I've never been snowboarding, actually."

"No way. You've never been snowboarding?" I was totally surprised.

Jason looked down and spoke so quietly I could barely hear him. "I dunno, I guess I just never had a snowboard or anything."

Boy, did I feel stupid. It hadn't even occurred to me that maybe Jason couldn't snowboard not because he didn't want to, but because he just never had the chance.

"Do you want to try it?"

Now it was Jason's turn to give the *Are you kidding?* look.

"No, really. My dad owns ATS Sports and I bet he could loan out a snowboard for the day. And I'm no expert teacher or anything, but I'm pretty good. It'd be so much fun! How 'bout it?"

Suddenly a huge smile burst onto Jason's face. But before he had a chance to say anything there was a knock on the door. Jason turned pale and looked as nervous as he had back at The Sweet Life. "Jason, is Avery in there?" It was Bonnie.

"Yeah!" he called. I bit my lip as we waited for the door to open. But it didn't. Jason looked at Ollie like he was silently warning him to keep his beak closed!

"Avery, your dad just called," Bonnie called through the door. "Would you two come inside and call him back?"

"Be right there!" I replied. We listened tensely as Bonnie's footsteps hesitated outside the shed door, then finally headed off in the direction of the house. *Phew!* Jason looked at me and smiled with relief. I felt the same way. We were *this close* to having Bonnie discover his mega-huge secret.

"Wow." Jason breathed a sigh of relief. "Bonnie never comes down here. She said it could be my private place."

I looked down at my watch. "Oh, no! I totally lost track of time. I should have called my dad as soon as I got here! I hope he's not too worried."

Jason straightened up the room and carefully locked up the shed before we dashed back into the house.

"Was my dad mad?" I blurted out when we got inside.

Bonnie hesitated. Ick . . . I really hoped I wasn't in trouble. "He said Kazie told him you were probably here, but he does want you home soon. I told him I'd give you a ride."

"Thanks, Bonnie." I saw my mug of hot chocolate sitting on the counter . . . just as Bonnie promised. I really wanted to stay longer and drink it and talk to Jason some more, but I was probably already in hot water. Enough adventures for one night. Bonnie got her purse and Jason and I followed her to the door.

"Is it okay if I come, Bonnie?" he asked.

"Well . . ." Bonnie started.

Just then Frankie appeared in the door to the hallway. "You have to stay here, Jason. It's too late to be out," Frankie said in a serious voice. I wanted to laugh. He sounded like a parent.

"Would you mind . . . ?" Bonnie mouthed so only Jason and I could see.

Jason held up his hand for Frankie to slap. "Okay, buddy. I'm not going anywhere."

"Yay!" Frankie jumped up and down and clapped. "Let's go play Monopoly. C'mon. You're gonna be the thimble." Frankie grabbed one of Jason's hands and started to lead him out of the room.

"You want to hang out tomorrow?" Jason called over his shoulder.

"Sure! You can meet Marty."

10

Transition

Please don't let Kazie and Andie still be here, I thought to myself when we pulled into Dad's driveway. Just in case I was in a teeny, tiny bit of trouble—the last thing I wanted was for Andie and Kazie to witness it.

"Thanks so much for the ride, Bonnie," I said.

"You're welcome. Stop by our place anytime. You know . . ." Bonnie began quietly, "I'm glad you came over tonight. Jason's a great kid, but he's so shy . . . he ends up spending a lot of time alone. It's tough to be the new kid somewhere, and I'm glad he's finally found a friend."

"Me too," I told her. I was definitely not the new kid in Telluride, technically speaking, but for some reason having Kazie around made me feel like I was . . . and it wasn't fun. But hanging out with Radley, Ollie, and especially Jason, well, that was awesome. "Tell Jason thanks for me. I'll see you around, Bonnie!" I exclaimed as I hopped out of the car.

Uh-oh. The first face I saw when the door to my house

opened was Dad's, and it wasn't a happy one. But the faces behind him—Kazie, Andie, and (ugh) Farkle—were way worse. And everyone was giving me the exact same look—the one that went: *Avery Madden . . . tsk, tsk, tsk.* Except Kazie. She wouldn't look at me at all.

The room was so quiet that I could literally hear the zipper buzzing as I took off my coat. *Zzzzzzzzzip.* "Hey, everybody, what's up?" I asked. "Have a good night . . . ?" Rats! My happy talk wasn't making people forget they were mad at me. If anything, Dad's frown only got bigger.

"Avery," he said, "why did you leave Kazie like that in the ice cream shop? Don't you think you might owe her an apology?"

Not really, I thought, remembering the racing joke she pulled on the way there. But I figured there was no way around apologizing, especially with Dad right there. "I'm sorry, Kazie. And I'm really sorry, Dad. I meant to call you when I got to Jason's but I totally forgot when I saw his, um . . . ferret. Yeah, that's it, his ferret, and I just forgot." Well, that was believable . . . NOT! Kazie rolled her eyes and Dad glanced at Andie.

"She's all right. And that's what matters, Jake," Andie told Dad quietly.

"Yeah! I'm fine. I was fine all along . . ." I agreed, suddenly liking this Andie lady a little bit more.

Dad nodded at Andie. "Thanks for sticking around. I think I need to have a one-on-one with my daughter now."

"Okay. I'll see you in the morning," Andie said with a smile. She put on her coat. Then, my night went from weird to weirder. She actually *kissed Dad on the cheek*. And just when I thought things couldn't get any worse, *he kissed her right back.*

Kazie groaned and made a gagging sound but I just looked away. He was my dad, for crying out loud! At least Kazie and I were on the same page about kissing parents.

"Good night, Avery. It was nice to see you again," Andie said.

"You too," I muttered. If she thought I was kissing her cheek she had another think coming. No way, José! Kazie stomped off and let the door slam behind her. I was just happy to see Farkle the Franken-cat leave so Marty could finally relax.

I thought it would be a relief to finally have Dad back to myself. Unfortunately, he seemed just as annoyed.

"I'm so, so sorry, Dad. I promise it was an accident. I swear on . . . on snowboarding!" That made a smile creep onto Dad's face. A little one, but still, better than nothing.

"I know you're growing up, Avery, and I'm not exactly sure what your mom's rules are in Boston, but here in Telluride you need to let me know where you are. Especially at night. Kazie always tells Andie exactly where she is and who she's with. I expect the same from you."

I knew Dad was right, but I didn't like being compared to Crazie Kazie. To tell the truth, I was sick of her name coming up all the time. Besides, it was an honest mistake. And that mistake might not have even happened if Kazie'd been nicer to me at The Sweet Life. But how was I supposed to tell Dad that?

Dad started washing the dishes in the sink and handed

them to me to dry. "So tell me about your new friend," he said. "What's his name . . . Jason? From what Kazie says, he's kind of a man of mystery . . . if you will." Dad nudged me in the arm.

I stared hard at the dish I was drying.

"Avery?" Dad prompted me.

"What?" I sounded startled. I wanted to tell Dad about Jason but the words just weren't coming. It was embarrassing, and I wasn't sure why. "I don't know. He's nice. He likes animals, like me. He doesn't know a lot of kids here yet."

"Kazie loves animals," Dad pointed out. *Who cares what Crazie Kazie thinks about animals?* Why was Dad obsessed with making sure that Kazie and I liked all the same things? "She did bring Farkle. Marty must be happy to have a new friend," Dad added with a wink. We looked at each other and burst out laughing.

"Pleeeease, Dad. Farkle and Marty? You've got to be kidding me. That's like me hanging out with Anna and Joline. It's just not gonna happen."

Dad laughed. He knew all about the Queens of Mean. Farkle was the Feline King of Mean—that was for sure! Dad gave me a big hug. "I want you to feel completely at home here . . . always. Just make sure that next time you tell me before you go somewhere, okay?"

"Okay," I promised. "Dad . . . there's one more thing."

"Yeah?"

"Well, I think that it would be a lot easier for Jason to make friends in Telluride if he knew how to snowboard. But he hasn't lived here very long and he's never tried it before. I know that snowboarding can be expensive . . . so I was thinking maybe there's some way we could help him? I know he'd want to help out in return." Jason didn't seem like the type to accept a handout. "I was just thinking he could borrow a snowboard . . . like for the day or something just to try it out."

Dad shrugged. "It's no problem. I can always use an extra hand with inventory. He can come in the morning at nine a.m. But are you sure that this is what Jason wants, Avery?"

"Please, Dad! He lives in Colorado! Every kid in Colorado needs to snowboard. That'd be like . . . like, um . . . like living in Hawaii and not being able to surf."

Dad rolled his eyes, but he was totally not mad anymore. "Okay, Avery."

"Or like living in Boston and hating the Red Sox."

"Don't even go there!" Dad laughed and started pushing me to the stairs to get ready for bed.

But I was just getting started. "Or living in the North Pole and hating reindeer. Or—"

"I get the picture," he said and plopped a furry little ball in my arms.

"Marty!"

Marty made a yelpy noise that I'd never heard before. He kept looking frantically around the room and then up at me. "Don't worry, little dude," I assured him. "Farkle's gone. We're safe now."

"Okay, Avery, good night," Dad said and tried to send me off with a hug, but I was too quick and dodged it instead.

"Time out! Can I call Jason super quick before I go to bed? Please?"

Dad tapped his watch, but handed me the phone and a phonebook to look up Fred and Bonnie Hulbert. I flipped through the pages and crossed my fingers that I had the right one. After three rings, someone picked up.

"Herr-ow," said a kid at the other end.

"Um, hi. Is Jason there?"

"Who is it?" asked the kid.

"It's Avery . . . is this Frankie?"

"Mooooooom!" he suddenly shouted, and then I heard a *"BEEP! BEEP! BEEP!"* He hung up on me. Whoa.

I sighed and waited a minute before clicking on the phone again to redial the number. But when I did there wasn't any dial tone.

"Hello?" This voice still belonged to a boy, but older this time.

"Jason?" I asked hopefully.

"Avery?"

I laughed. "Whoa! It's so weird that you called! I just tried to call you but Frankie accidentally hung up on me. At least, I think it was an accident."

"Actually . . . I figured it was you when I saw Madden on the caller ID."

Duh! "Oh, right." I took a deep breath and cut to the chase. "All right, you remember how I was telling you about snowboarding tonight?"

"Uh-huh."

"Okay. Well, I was talking to my dad and he said he needed some help with inventory this weekend. If you worked, he'd loan out a snowboard, and you could see what you think. We could even go tomorrow . . . if you want."

Silence.

"Jason?"

"Wow. That's really nice of you Avery, but . . ."

Oh, no. Was he offended that I was trying to offer him a job? "If you don't, that's okay too," I added quickly.

"No, I *do* . . . it's just that . . . well . . . I've never done it before. Could be a bad scene."

"Well you have to start somewhere, Jason. Don't you think it'd be more fun with me than some old know-it-all snowboarding instructor?"

"Okay," he said quietly, and then he gave a louder, "Okay!"

"Awesome!" I agreed. "My dad says you can start at nine. I'll stop by the store to get you after. Tell Ollie good night for me."

Jason was laughing. "Okay, I will. Bye, Avery," he said.

"Bye, Jason. Oh! And good night to Radley, too."

Part Two
Major Pow-Wow

CHAPTER
11

Air-to-Fakie

That night, I had a Snurf-tastic dream about the competition. It went like this: It was snowing hard, and I was totally on fire as I executed three perfect flips on the halfpipe. The next thing I knew, I was standing on the platform to accept my FIRST PLACE trophy. All the kids from The Sweet Life were there cheering. Sitting at the judges' table holding up scorecards that read "10" were Dad, Donnie Keeler, and Jason (I know, weird). I was super excited, waving my trophy in the air and shouting, "Snurfer! Snurfer! Snurfer!" when suddenly a drop of rain hit my face. I tried to keep shouting, but the rain was coming down in buckets. I felt my hair sticking to my cheek and when I wiped it away I realized I was awake and it wasn't rain at all . . . it was dog slobber. Marty!

I sat up and gave the little dude a hug. "Goooood morning, Marty Man." Marty leaped out of the bed and barked at the window. The sun was shining through the curtains, and it was insanely bright. I looked at the clock on my nightstand. Yikes! It was already nine o'clock. Dad and Jason were definitely at the store by now, and Dad probably let me sleep in. Mucho cool of him, but now it was time to get up. "Thanks, Marty. I totally can't waste another second. I have a Snurfer to practice for!"

I looked outside as soon as I hopped out of bed. "Wowza!" I exclaimed. It had snowed . . . a lot! At least that part of the dream came true. There was a thick white blanket over everything—all the cars, roofs, and trees. It was so bright, I had to squint to see clearly. "Perfect pow-pow here I come!"

One of my top-ten sports rules is, no matter what, dress for comfort. Even though blue was definitely my fave color for basically everything, today I was going to wear my purple snowboarding turtleneck. Okay, I know the BSG would probably be thinking, *Purple? Avery? No way!* But believe me, this was one Snurf-worthy shirt. Dad got it for me last Christmas and it was made of one hundred percent mossbud fleece, so it totally breathed when I boarded, but it also kept me warm and cozy at the same time.

I rolled up my boarding pants and stuffed them in my backpack along with my gloves and wrist guards. Then I pulled my hair into a low side-ponytail so I could get my helmet on. I was ready to ride.

When I got downstairs I noticed a box on the kitchen table in dog bone wrapping paper. There was a note on it too. "Rise and shine, sleepyheads! Remember, breakfast is the most important meal of the day, so eat up! I'll see you at the store. And there's something special for Marty in the box."

"Wow, Marty, a present for you! Isn't Dad the best?" I would've let Marty open it, but he wasn't a very good unwrapper. (Trust me, the BSG tried before and it wasn't pretty . . . unless you were a big confetti fan.) So I tore off the paper and opened the box. Inside was a little blue Nordic sweater with the words "Snurfer Dog" knitted on the back. I held it up for Marty to see. "What do you think, pal? A real Snurfer sweater all for you! Pretty cool, huh?"

Marty sniffed at it and barked happily. Cute little Marty sweaters were Maeve's thing . . . NOT mine. I mean, come on! He's the Marty man . . . the M-Dawg. He's waaay too cool for cutesy-pootsy sweaters. But a *Snurfer* sweater—well, that was another story. Snurfer Marty was going to look like one put-together pooch, and boy, did he know it!

I took out a bowl for me and a bowl for Marty. His breakfast was obvious: kibbles, kibbles, and more kibbles. But what about mine? Dad was totally right . . . eating a good breakfast was *crucial* for a day of sweet boarding. Plain old cereal wasn't going to cut it.

First, I stuffed two pieces of thick wheat bread in the toaster. Then I grabbed a box of granola and some vanilla yogurt and poured them both in my bowl. I sliced a banana, an apple, some strawberries, and even sprinkled on blueberries. A yogurt parfait all for me! *Bing* went the toaster and up popped my toast—golden brown. After I smeared on butter and raspberry jam, the toast was super delicious smelling. Not too shabby, if I did say so myself . . . and I did. *Eat your heart out, Scott!* It was the perfect pre-mountain breakfast.

"Okay, widdew Marty, ready for a widdew walk?" I held up the Snurfer sweater. The lady on the plane would have loved widdew Marty in his cutesy-pie sweater.

Marty *arf*ed and trotted over to me. He must've loved the sweater too, because he popped his little head right inside! For Marty, that was huge. After I helped him get his paws through the armholes (a tricky operation), he took off prancing around the room. Marty looked like a total stud in his new outfit, and he couldn't wait to show it off. He was leaping and barking and going crazy while I put his leash on. When I checked out the window, I knew what was up. There was a dog coming around the corner—just about Marty's size, black and white with spiky fur. A very cool-looking dog.

"You want to make a new friend, don't you, Marty? New friends rock!" I thought of *my* new friend, Jason. We were going to have a blast snowboarding for sure. I grabbed my backpack, put on my big yellow coat (Okay, Scott's big yellow coat), and reached into the pocket for my ear warmer. *Oh, no!* It wasn't there. I checked the other pocket just to be sure and found NOTHING! I could've sworn I put it away there last night. What if I'd dropped it in the snow behind Jason's house? I knew I could always pick out a new ear warmer from Dad's store, no problem, but still . . . my ear warmer was a Kgirl original, and I wanted it back!

Marty looked at me with his big dog eyes. "Okay, okay, we'll go." I made a mental note to ask Jason about the ear warmer later.

The dog and his owner were on the sidewalk right in front of the house when we got outside. "Hi!" I called to the dude. He was wearing a red jacket and bright yellow hat. I couldn't see his eyes because of his sporty sunglasses (that sort of made him look like an insect!), but his nose was covered with freckles. "My dog wants to meet your dog, I think. He's new in town."

"Radical! Join the club," the guy said. He gave Marty a friendly rub on his head, then stood up and pulled off his hat. A huge blast of yellow hair puffed out. He pushed up his glasses to hold his crazy hair back. This dude was smiling real big like he knew an inside joke . . . but a joke that I was supposed to know too. It took me a second to figure out where I'd seen that hair before. Then I remembered— the cover of *Mountain Monthly*, my favorite snowboarding magazine.

"No way! You're . . . you're . . . the Egg! The Golden Egg! Donnie Keeler!"

"'Fraid so," he said with a laugh. "I guess you're a boarder, too."

"Wow! How'd you know?"

Donnie Keeler bent down and patted Marty. "'Cause only snowboarders know who I am off the slopes. Which is totally cool. I like that the only people who know me are the real fans."

I tried to think of something smart to say so he'd know I was a real fan, but the only thing that came out was, "Hah. Yeah." *Hah. Yeah? Good one, Ave.*

"You can call me DK, by the way," he said and held out a gloved hand for me to shake. "And this guy"—he nodded at his dog—"is Crud."

I laughed and shook his glove with mine. I would have

to explain to Marty later that **crud** was a snowboarding word that meant inconsistent snow . . . you know, like icy or slushy. Crud snow is NOT sweet to board on, AND Crud was probably the funniest dog name in the history of dog names. "I'm Avery Madden," I said. "It's awesome to meet you."

"Wait . . . Madden? By any chance, is your dad Jake the Snurfman?"

"Yup."

"No way! I'm judging the Snurfer Competition."

"I know," I said proudly. How sweet was it that I already had the inside scoop on what was going on in Telluride? "We're so excited that you're here. I'm going to be in the competition."

DK saluted me. "Sweet. Good luck little Snurfette."

I laughed and covered my mouth. No one had ever called me "Snurfette" before, but I really liked it. Imagine the Snurfer loudspeakers: "It's a bird . . . it's a plane . . . NO . . . it's Snurfette! Boy, can she shred!" Oh, yeah. It definitely had a nice ring to it.

"So what kind of dog is Crud?" I asked DK. "At first I thought he was a terrier, but his fur looks more like a collie."

"Right on! Crud's a Border Jack—a mix of a Border collie and a Jack Russell terrier. Boarders and Borders just get each other, you know? Who's this guy?" He scratched Marty's belly and Marty rolled around in the snow, loving every minute of it.

"This is Marty. My friends and I found him in a garbage can and decided to adopt him. He's a mutt just like Crud, but we don't know what kind. I like to call him a Serengeti Wallaby, 'cause who knows—he could be from Africa, or Australia, or anywhere!"

Marty and Crud the Border Jack were playing in the snow piled up beside the sidewalk. There were so many things I wanted to ask the Golden Egg—like especially if he had any secret shred-tastic boarding tips! Instead, here we were just talking about our dogs, like any old normal people in Telluride. I really wanted to stay and talk some more, but I knew Dad was waiting for me at the store.

"Well, it was nice to meet you, DK, but I gotta run. I'm going to my dad's store to help out this morning."

"Wait, before you go . . . do you know anywhere around here where I could get a decent breakfast? I'm craving a huuuge waffle! It's what my mom always makes before I go boarding." With his messy hair and tanned cheeks, DK looked like he was a teenager. Then I remembered—DK *was* a teenager. I read in *Mountain Monthly* that DK was just seventeen! Five years older than me . . . practically the same age as Scott. And he traveled to all these places by himself. Wow. I totally understood why he'd want a waffle to remind him of home. I searched my brain for the perfect place.

It was honestly weird. When I looked around—like *magic*—there was this sign for a restaurant that I'd never seen before. "Come Visit Maggie's: Home of the Famous Waffle Mountain." A new breakfast place in Telluride! Was luck on my side this morning or what?

We tied up Marty and Crud outside and walked in. "Wow, this place looks amaaaazing, Snurfette!"

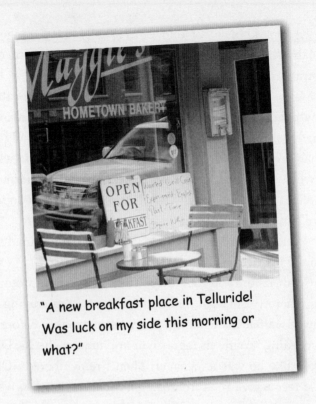

"A new breakfast place in Telluride! Was luck on my side this morning or what?"

The restaurant smelled like coffee, a hot griddle, and warm maple syrup. It was hopping inside, full of people who looked like marshmallows walking around in their puffy jackets, filling up before a long day at the mountain.

"Are you going to get some waffles?" DK asked.

"Gee, I wanna stay, but . . ." Just then I noticed a rack of postcards near the door. Good thing I had Charlotte's key ring with the tiny pen on it. If I mailed some postcards today, they'd get to Brookline before I got home. "Well, maybe just a quick hot chocolate," I agreed. "I've got some serious postcard writing to do!"

"All right! Rad!"

I went over to the rack to pick out cards, and DK hopped onto a stool at the counter. They were spinners—like at Fat Alley. (To be an awesome Colorado restaurant, you gotta get the spinning chairs!) I grabbed four postcards that I knew the BSG would love: Ajax Peak from a plane, the shops on Main Street, a huge avalanche, and the Telluride Film Festival. It didn't really matter who got which card . . . except one. I was definitely going to give the film festival card to Maeve!

DK ordered me a hot chocolate, and it was on the counter waiting for me when I reached the counter.

"What do you think?" I asked, showing him the cards I picked out.

"All very righteous," he said approvingly. "Are these for your friends at home?"

"Yup. They're in Brookline. They made me promise to write to them this week."

"Right on. So what are you going to write about?" asked DK.

I thought about this for a sec and sipped the hot chocolate. Ouch! It was burning hot. DK laughed when I made a dive for my ice water. I gulped it and even threw some ice cubes in the hot chocolate for good measure. Then I started scribbling on the avalanche card:

Dear Isabel,

Thought of you 'cause of this cool picture! I boarded yesterday. It was soooo awesome to be on the slopes again!

Then I had to stop. What I really wanted to write about was meeting Jason and Ollie the hawk . . . and now hanging out with DK. But if the BSG got a postcard from Avery Madden about *two guys*, even if they were cool guys, they'd think I'd been abducted by aliens! Besides, I wasn't excited in a Maeve-crush kind of way. Jason was awesome because he was raising a wild hawk, and Donnie Keeler, well—celebrity snowboarder? That was a no-brainer!

DK noticed me staring hard at the postcard and chewing the end of my pen. "Boarder's block?" he joked.

"Kinda," I admitted.

He nodded. "I hear that. When I first went pro, all my friends wanted to hear about were the shows and the competitions. But the best parts of my trips were always these random stories and not stuff I could explain in postcards. Like once, I was so tired after a day of practice that I fell asleep standing in the hotel elevator."

"No way!"

"Way. And you haven't heard the best part . . . I didn't wake up till my head slid and set off the fire alarm button. Now that's funny stuff. But I don't know if it's postcard worthy. Friends want to hear about the action, the competitions, you know?"

Not my friends, I thought. The BSG loved letters from the heart. I sipped my hot chocolate. Now that it was a little cooler, I could taste its yumminess. But it was still no Montoya's.

DK looked over my shoulder. "Maybe I can help?" He picked up the pen.

"Sure!" I slid a postcard over to him and watched. First,

he drew a mountain with two stick-figure people at the bottom holding the leashes of two stick-figure dogs. (My kind of artwork!) The taller of the figures had a big puff of hair, and the other had a low side-ponytail. Hah! He was obviously drawing us! Under his picture he wrote "Master of Crud" and under mine he wrote "Snurfette." He signed, "Boogie on, DK" and left a space for me.

"Your turn," he said.

I wrote, "Miss you! Having an awesome time on the slopes. Love, Avery!" Wow. Wait till the BSG found out that their cards had been doodled on and signed by the Golden Egg himself! Even if they didn't know much about snowboarding celebs, they'd understand how cool this was. We finished up with Maeve's card just in time for DK's breakfast.

"The Waffle Mountain?" said the waiter, sliding a plate in front of DK. It was, honest-to-goodness, the biggest stack of waffles I'd ever laid eyes on. There were three Belgian waffles, all equally thick, but the bottom one was the biggest. It looked like a little earthquake had just created a small mountain of dough right in the middle of Maggie's.

"That's the sweetest mountain I've ever seen," DK whispered to me. "Too bad I left my board in my truck."

I laughed and then stopped when I spotted the clock on the wall. It was already ten. I had to jet! Too bad I couldn't stick around to see Waffle Mountain devoured. "I really have to run now," I told DK. "Thanks so much for your help."

"Hey, no prob, Snurfette. Tell your pops hi for me!"

I slurped down the rest of my hot chocolate and left two dollars on the counter. DK picked it up and put it back in my hand.

"My treat," he said. "If it wasn't for the Snurfman, I wouldn't get to be in Telluride in the first place."

"Thanks!" I exclaimed. "See you on the mountain!" And I bolted out of the store, barely slowing down to untie Marty and pull him along after me.

I jogged all the way to ATS Sports with a huge smile frozen on my face, and it wasn't because of the cold weather. I couldn't help that I was still ridiculously excited from my close encounter of the snowboard-star-kind!

But that smile disappeared the second I opened the door to ATS. The first person I saw inside was Kazie. She was slumped over the counter by the register and staring into space—totally zoned out. And she didn't look too thrilled to see me.

"Hi, what's up?" I asked. Might as well try to be friendly, right?

"Nothing." Kazie groaned. "Absolutely nothing. There was no reason for me to come to work this morning."

I looked at her strangely. "Why not?" I asked.

"Someone took over my job," she informed me in a cold voice.

Just then the door to the back room opened, and Jason walked out with a box of ski goggles in his arms. "Hey, Avery!" he called.

"Hi, Jason! This is Marty."

"Nice to meet you, Marty." Jason rubbed Marty's nose

and let Marty slobber as much as he wanted. M-Dawg was so friendly he was already giving Jason wet kisses all over his feet . . . and Jason didn't mind a bit!

"Sorry I took so long, but guess who I met on the way here?" I asked as I helped Jason unload. "I'll give you a clue: Think famous."

"Umm . . ." Jason furrowed his brows, which made me notice his super-blue eyes again. *Stop staring before he thinks you're a total weirdo!* I told myself and concentrated on the goggle project instead. "Tom Cruise?" he asked.

"Nope."

"Doesn't he live around here . . . ?"

I shook my head. "I dunno. Even if he did . . . movie stars are my friend Maeve's thing, not mine. Guess again."

Jason shrugged. "I give up. Who?"

"Donnie Keeler!" The blank look on Jason's face told me that he had *a lot* to learn about snowboarding. "You know . . . the Olympic gold medalist . . . ?"

"DONNIE KEELER?" Two yellow pigtails shot up from behind the register. Today Kazie was wearing her hair in braids with orange ribbons twisted in as an extra touch. "You met the Golden Egg?" Kazie hurtled out from behind the counter and headed right toward us. I was afraid she was going to topple me, but she stopped right before that happened.

"Well, yeah. You know he's here for the Snurfer."

"Sure, but . . . why was he just *walking around* Telluride? He should come HERE to ATS and . . . and . . . meet ME!"

It's probably crazy fans like you that DK's afraid of! I thought, but I didn't tell Kazie that. Jason was looking at us like we'd both lost it. "He's just a chill guy, Kazie. We got waffles from Maggie's, that new diner. Well, *he* got waffles. I just got a hot chocolate and wrote some postcards." Kazie looked like her head was going to pop off! Then I remembered something. "Oh, no!" I cried and smacked my forehead.

"What's wrong?" asked Jason.

I'd been in such a rush to leave Maggie's that I had forgotten to take the postcards with me. I'd just have to tell the BSG about the adventure myself. "Never mind," I replied. But the postcards reminded me of something else that was missing. "Hey, you haven't seen my ear warmer by any chance, have you?"

"Ear warmer?" Jason asked.

I grabbed one off the shelf and waved it. "It looks kinda like this . . ."

"Oh, you mean your headband. Nope. Haven't seen it since last night. But I'll stay on the lookout."

I shrugged. "Well, thanks anyway. Hey, are you almost done around here?"

Jason thought for a moment. "Um . . . there are kind of a lot of boxes that I have to count and stuff . . ."

"Which can wait till another day." Dad stepped out from the back room just in time. "Don't you think it's about time you kids hit the slopes?"

I punched the air, suddenly psyched to start the day. "Really? Thanks, Dad!"

"Hey, don't thank me. Thank Jason. He's a hard worker," Dad said, and looked at Jason with a serious face. "Jason, what would you think about a semipermanent job here on the weekends?"

Jason looked down, embarrassed and proud at the same time. "Really, Mr. M? That'd be great . . ."

The Snurfman strikes again! My dad was one awesome dude. Dad brushed his hands together. "Then it's settled."

"Okay, I'm going to pick out a board for you," I decided. I knew just the one—blue sky background with a brown hawk on the bottom. Jason's eyes got huge the minute he saw it.

Dad jingled his keys. "Ride to the mountain?" he offered with a smile.

"Sweet!" I exclaimed, high-fiving him. I looked out the window and took a deep breath. *Telluride Ski Resort, here we come!*

12

Goofy-Footed

I can't believe I wiped out again. Just when I thought I was getting the hang of this!" Jason was lying flat on his back on the **bunny slope**. "Remind me one more time why I agreed to go snowboarding?"

"This isn't snowboarding," I said, sliding back and forth on my board to stay balanced. "This is falling . . . and everybody falls on their first day. You've got to chill, dude."

Jason tried to get up and slipped. He tried to get up again, slipped again, and sighed. "Forget it!" He sat dejectedly on the snow as other kids skied and boarded past us.

"Come on, Jason. You're doing awesomely, I swear!" I reached out and helped Jason get back on his feet.

"Well then, why are all the rugrats going so much faster than me? They look like they're Frankie's age."

"Younger, probably." I scanned the little balls of color flying by. "I dunno. Kids always ski fast. They don't have any fear, you know? If they fall, it's not far for them to go. Trust me—I'm a shortie. I know these things."

Jason sighed and brushed the snow off his coat. "Okay. What next?"

"Follow me," I said. I slowly carved my way to the bottom of the hill. My path was like a long, curvy snake. I kept checking over my shoulder to make sure Jason was okay. But actually, he was better than okay. Jason was on his feet and boarding. It was so cool.

We got to the bottom and I slowed to a stop. Jason fell over backward again—that was how all beginners stopped. "Ahhh!" he groaned.

"Sweeet run!" I high-fived Jason, and he smiled. I could tell he was having fun again. We rode the lift back up and I let Jason lead the way to the bottom. After five perfect (well . . . almost perfect) runs, Jason was getting the hang of it. He even started to show off a little bit by snowboarding backward. That's when I knew it was time.

"Are you shreddy for the gondola?" I asked.

"Am I *what* for the *what*?"

Oops. I kept forgetting that Jason didn't know all my boarding expressions yet. "How about trying a **green circle** slope?" I wanted to make sure he felt comfortable before we went on a harder slope.

Jason shrugged. "You think I'm ready?"

"Sure! The question is . . . do *you* think you're ready?"

Jason didn't say a word, but smiled and took off, sliding right down to the gondola line. Wow! My lessons were paying off.

We got in line behind a group of guys. They looked like

they were our age but they didn't say hi to us. They were too busy messing around. One kid picked up a handful of snow and slipped it into the back of another one's coat. "Hey, quit it!" the second kid screeched, squirming to get the snow out. I laughed—that was seriously the oldest trick in the book. My older brothers used to get me with it plenty of times . . . that is, until I learned how to get revenge!

I looked at Jason and rubbed my hands together mischievously. "Don't even think about it," he warned. Smart of him . . . definitely.

Jason didn't look too thrilled when we had to share a gondola with these kids, though. They shoved their snowboards into the side and hopped right on. I put mine in too and stepped back for Jason. Uh-oh. Jason was still stuck in his bindings!

"Yo, hurry up, Jason! You're going to miss it!" called one of the guys. Weird—I guess they did know him after all. The chairlift attendant helped Jason out, but by the time he was done, Jason's cheeks were bright red. He slipped into the car just before the door slammed shut.

"Nice save," I breathed. Jason's expression didn't look too happy anymore.

The three guys sat there without saying a word—not even a "hey"—as the cable yanked us high above the trees. Jason stared silently out the window.

"So Jas, what brings you 'round these parts?" one of the kids finally asked. It was the one who played the snow-down-the-back trick.

"Yeah . . . where's your pet rat?" asked another. They cracked up.

Jason glowered at the kid. "He's not a rat, he's a ferret," he muttered.

The boys chuckled. "I thought you didn't dig shredding," challenged the first one.

Jason shrugged. "Maybe I do."

"Yeah," I added. "He's allowed to change his mind, you know."

"What do you know! It's kiddie day at Telluride!" said the third kid . . . to me. I didn't care when the BSG teased me about my height, but these three random dudes? Noooo way.

I slapped my knee. "Wow, that's hilarious! Because I'm short, right? I look like a little kid! Oh, boy, that's a good one. How original!" I pretended to laugh hysterically and then stopped mid-laugh. Now I *really* had their attention. Jason's, too!

I leaned in close and squinted my eyes to show I meant business. "Listen. I might be small but that doesn't mean I can't shred."

Two of the guys seemed a little nervous, but the one in the middle leaned in and squinted too. "Oh, yeah? Well if you're so great, then why haven't we seen you here before?"

"Yeah!" the other guys mumbled.

"'Cause . . . I'm not from here. I'm from Boston," I replied. "I'm visiting my dad for the Snurfer Competition."

All the guys burst out laughing. "That's what *you* think. No grommets allowed in this competition! Snurfman rules!"

I was just about to set them straight when Jason blurted, "Well, guess what? Her dad IS the Snurfman!"

Whoa. That was a surprise. I glanced at him and smiled. He smiled back.

One of the guys whispered something to another and then said, "Your dad's the Snurfman? No way. You don't look anything like the Snurfman!"

I felt my throat tense up. I took a deep breath and tried to remember to do what Mom always taught me: be proud of who I was. "Duh, I'm adopted," I said coolly.

They shut up instantly. "Sorry," murmured the one who made the comment.

"It's okay," I told him. It wasn't *totally* okay . . . but I knew that sometimes people said things without thinking about them. I mean, I did it all the time. "I'm Korean-American," I explained. "My parents got me when I was a baby."

"My cousin Lydia's adopted," said the kid in the middle. "I don't even think about it most of the time."

"See, that's what it's like for me too," I replied.

After that no one was mean anymore. The boys asked me about the Snurfer and being from Boston, and even though Jason didn't say much he definitely looked more comfortable than he had back in the chairlift line.

The gondola pulled into the station and the boys jumped out first. "Nice to meet you, Avery. See you in school, Jason. Later, dudes!" they called and boarded away. *Not so bad,* I thought, once you talked to them for more than a minute.

"Hey . . . thanks," I said to Jason as we strapped on our bindings.

He looked confused. "For what?"

"You know . . . telling those guys about my dad."

He shrugged. "No prob. I . . . I know what it's like. I mean, when you're new you get used to people asking a lot of questions. It gets annoying after a while."

"Totally." Wow, and I thought it was awkward to answer questions when I had a mom and dad and brothers and everything . . . what about Jason? And Frankie? Suddenly I wasn't so worried about Jason being able to make it down the mountain. He was definitely brave—no doubt about it!

"All right, you ready to go on your first real shredding run?"

Jason pulled his goggles over his eyes and gave me the thumbs-up.

We started out slowly, and I let Jason lead. That way if he fell I'd be able to board over and help him up. Jason didn't fall though. That is, until we reached the halfway point. He toppled to a stop, laughing the whole time.

"This is totally awesome. No wonder everyone around here is obsessed with this sport!"

"Told you!" I replied. "Shredding's the be—" Suddenly a wave of snow sprayed over me, and because I was talking, I got a royal mouthful. "Blech!" I spat and wiped my face.

When the ice fog settled I saw a girl in a magenta coat standing there with a huge smile on her face. Kazie. I should've known. "'Sup shredders?" she asked. "You ready to race, Jase? Hah! Race Jase. That rhymes!"

Jason's face was red . . . this time almost as red as the snowboards that Kazie and I were riding on.

"I, uh, we're still . . ." he stammered. *Back to shy-Jason mode*, I thought.

"Not yet, Kazie," I said. "We're chilling this morning." I pushed up my goggles and looked at her straight in the eye. Actually, I had to look *up* at her. She seemed like a combination of Maeve and Katani in her snowboarding outfit. The pink, well, that was Maeve for sure. But the ribbons and little patches she had sewn on from all the places she'd been . . . that was Kgirl. Then there was the way she boarded. Like a pro. Kazie was pretty much good at everything . . . and she knew it, too. How intimidating!

She was smiling from ear to ear. "What are you . . . chicken? Bok, bok, bok." Kazie made her arms into wings and did a little chicken dance on her board. She was talking to me now . . . not Jason. And Jason, beside me, was laughing a little bit. Did he think she was funny?

"Please. I'd race you any day. But no racing on the job," I told her. "We're in the middle of a lesson." Period—the end. I wasn't going to let Kazie spoil this.

"Whatever. Looking good, Jason. Nice moves." Kazie gave him a thumbs-up, which made him smile. "Yo, Avery—see you on the pipe . . . if you dare." And Kazie slipped off, flying over a jump as she sped away. As she did she tucked the **tail** of her board, grabbed with her left hand, and did a perfect 180-degree spin.

"She's really good, isn't she?" Jason said, staring after her. Uh-oh. Another member of the Crazie Kazie Fan Club? Then he said something that scared me even more. "Can we go to the Superpipe?"

"You . . . want to ride the . . . PIPE?" The Superpipe was

going to be the run for the Snurfer! How could I tell Jason that he was sooo not ready for the pipe without hurting his feelings? "Don't you think that this run might be a little better for you? Remember, it's still your first day . . ."

"No way! I'm not going ride it. I kind of wanted to see you ride it . . . actually."

"Oh." Then I had a thought. "And Kazie, right?"

Jason shook his head and looked at the ground. "I mean, she's good, but . . ."

I didn't give him time to answer. "Fine. We'll go." I'd known Crazie Kazie for like two days and *already* I could tell that she had to be the center of attention. Well, if Jason wanted to watch her showoff-y tricks, fine. I didn't wait to see if he was ready or not. I slid off—FAST.

"Hey, Avery, wait up!" Jason shouted after me.

I stopped and turned. Just as I did, a little boy on skis cut right in front of Jason. "Heeeeere I come!" the kid squealed. He was bent over with his little poles tucked right under his arms and going faster than a speeding bullet. This type of thing drove boarders crazy.

I jumped to the side and avoided him, but Jason wasn't so lucky. When the kid cut him off it sent him totally out of control.

"Ahhhh!" he cried. He was slipping right toward me. "Avery, look out!"

One second I looked up and the next—*BAM!* My head hit the snow and I felt something heavy on top of my lower half. I was glad I was wearing a helmet! "Ouch . . ." I moaned and opened my eyes. "Jason?"

Jason awkwardly rolled off of my legs as fast as he

could with his feet still strapped into the board. He looked totally embarrassed. "Oh, geesh. I'm sorry, Avery." He shook his head and brushed the snow out of the cracks of his coat. "Aw, man . . . just when I thought I was getting the hang of this, I almost killed my teacher."

"Hey, don't worry about it." I suddenly felt kind of weird lying on the ground so close to Jason. On top of that, I also felt guilty that I'd boarded away instead of waiting for him.

Jason kept apologizing as he brushed the snow out of his hair. He looked everywhere but at me. "I'm really, really sorry."

"It wasn't your fault. You were **blindsided**. I blame the **Knee Rocket**."

Jason scrunched his eyebrows and stopped brushing. "Knee Rocket?"

"Oh, yeah. Little kids who can't stop skiing until they hit something. Bad news for boarders. But they're sooo adorable," I joked. We both laughed, and then suddenly Jason stopped.

"Hey, Avery . . . Kazie's really good," Jason began. Uh-oh. There it was—the annoyed feeling coming back. "And I was thinking," he continued, "maybe you should be at the pipe practicing for the Snurfer without worrying about helping me. The Snurfer's in two days, remember?"

"I'll be fine." But the truth was—I knew Jason was right. Kazie was good . . . and I was rusty. If I wanted to have any chance of placing at all in the competition, I should be practicing hardcore.

"That's why I thought maybe we could go to the halfpipe," Jason explained.

Wow. He was thinking of me after all—not Kazie. I opened my mouth to tell him that a promise was a promise when I felt another blast of snow hit my face.

"Okay, listen, I don't know what your problem is—" I looked up. "DAD?"

"Whoa, Mr. M! You really got us!" Jason laughed.

There he was: the Snurfman himself—bright blue jester cap and all. "What are you doing here?" I asked.

"Thought I'd take the newest member of the ATS team out for a lunch on the slopes. On the company. I could really use a cheeseburger right now. What do you say, Jason?" Dad quickly looked at me and winked. I knew just what he was up to. He was giving me a chance to go practice.

"Really, Mr. M? That'd be great! I'm starved. What about you, Avery?"

"Not yet," I said. "I think I'm going to try to squeeze in a few more runs before lunch, if that's okay."

"Fine by me," Dad said. "As long as Jason's okay with having a substitute teacher for a little bit."

"Yeah! And Avery, this'll give you a chance to hit the pipe after all." Jason looked relieved.

"Good idea." Dad winked at me again. "But first . . ." He reached into his coat pocket and pulled out a black case. "Picture time!"

I liked getting my picture taken. Most girls pretended to hate it, but come on. Who didn't secretly love seeing a picture of themselves? "C'mon, Jason. Do what I'm doing. It'll be funny!"

Jason shook his head. "No, thanks."

Dad motioned for him to get in the picture, and Jason stood there stiffly.

"Smile, guys. This is Jason's first time on the slopes, remember? Now get together and say 'fleas!'"

"Fleas?" Jason whispered.

"Yeah . . . my dad thinks it's funny," I told him.

"One, two, three," counted Dad.

"Fleas!"

CHAPTER

13

Hucker

A flying magenta coat was the first thing I saw when I got to the Superpipe. And there was the Flying Magenta Coat Fan Club—Tessa, Siobhan, and even the boys from the gondola—cheering every time Kazie went for a jump. And I had to admit, she really rocked it. *This mountain ain't big enough for the two of us!* I wanted to tell her.

"Hey, Avery! You made it!" Kazie practically screamed up the mountain.

"Ahoy to you too," I whispered under my breath.

I gave a little wave and waited for all the kids to go back to perfecting their own jumps. They didn't. Seemed like everyone wanted to know if the Snurfman's daughter was a decent boarder or not. I felt warm inside my coat. Really warm. It wasn't the spring snowboarding type of warm . . . it was the kind of warm when the teacher asked you a question and you didn't know the answer. Was I actually nervous? Yikes! This never happened to me on the slopes.

I stood at the top of the pipe and wondered what move I should do. If I tried to do a flip and looked bad, or worse yet, FELL, they'd think I was a total loser! Kazie'd probably laugh and then tell the story to Dad and Andie later, acting out the whole thing. Or worse, mention it in front of Jason. And knowing Kazie . . . she definitely would.

There was only one way to get through this and it wasn't going to be pretty. I pulled down my goggles and tipped my board forward into the bowl. "There she goes!" one of the kids shouted.

In a heartbeat I felt that rush. I really wanted to fly off of the jump, do a **backside 540** air and finish in a **McTwist**— one of my best tricks, but I couldn't risk messing up. Thankfully, I had a plan. I **hammered** all the way to the jump, took off, and soared, getting amazing air. I was going to be the **hucker** of the century on purpose. I raised my arms and wiggled them in the air. "Cowabunga dude! I'm out of controooooool!" Then I scrunched my body into a ball to do a little roll, but instead I hit the ground with a *SPLAT*. Wow, that hurt. Now I *really* couldn't breathe. When I finally stopped moving I was lying on my back.

Then I heard a noise. Laughing! Everyone was laughing—hard—but at least they were laughing *with* me . . . not *at* me. I jumped to my feet, took a deep breath, and bowed dramatically.

"Yeah, Avery! That was hilarious!" yelled the kids. They clapped, cheered, and whistled. Hah! My plan had worked perfectly. I could just see the headline: SNURFMAN'S DAUGHTER IS SNOWBOARDING COMEDY GENIUS!

Kazie sailed down the pipe on the opposite side, went

straight up the wall and into the air, and slid back down without turning—a **pop tart**. Then she rocketed off the other side and let out a loud, "Yeee haaw!" In the air, she rotated 90 degrees, flipped over, and rotated ANOTHER 90 degrees, landing right on her feet. It was as perfect a crippler as I had ever seen, even in the Olympics. She finished her halfpipe show with a midair flip, turning 90 degrees and landing backward—a **wet cat**. I gulped. There was no question . . . Kazie was a totally **hardcore** snowboarder—probably a shoo-in for Snurfer Champion.

Kazie slid beside me and shook her hair out of her helmet. I knew what that look on her face meant: *See, Avery, that's how it's done.*

I also knew how important it was to always be an all-star good sport, even if it meant *not* being the all-star. "Wow, Kazie," I said. "Nice crippler. That was **dice**."

Kazie shrugged. "That? Piece of cake. You know, Avery," Kazie said, flipping one of her famous ribbon braids over her shoulder. "The Snurfer might not be a sanctioned event—I mean, it's only a benefit—but still, it's not a clown competition. You actually have to *try*, Avery. And if you're not going to take it seriously, maybe you shouldn't bother entering. Or, you know, take some lessons for the rest of the day."

"Look, I was just having fun," I started to explain, but before I could get another word out, Siobhan called, "Hey, guys, there's live music at the Air Garden Yurt! Let's go!"

"Sweeeeet!" Kazie answered. She did an ollie and looked back at me with a really proud smile on her face. I didn't like it one bit.

"You coming, Avery?" asked Tessa. At least the rest of the kids thought I was funny. I wouldn't mind checking out the Air Garden Yurt, which was a big tent where a lot of the most rockin' bands played in Telluride. In fact, it would probably be really funny to get a picture of the tent to bring back to Henry Yurt. Henry, aka "the Yurtmeister," was class president back home in Boston and a total goofball. He'd probably *love* to see his name immortalized in a Telluride landmark . . . but today I had work to do. "Nah, go ahead. I'll see you guys later."

"See ya!" Kazie called and rode off immediately without looking back.

I grumbled and fumed walking back up to the top of the pipe. Nothing would give me more satisfaction than beating Kazie in the Snurfer. Of course, now I knew that was impossible . . . but hey . . . a girl could dream, right?

I closed my eyes and tried to visualize the jump—like my brothers told me to do when I was first learning how to board. I breathed in, zipped down the pipe, and sailed up the other side. With a *whoosh*, I was airborne. "It's a bird, it's a plane . . ." I shouted out loud and reached to grab the front of my board. "It's Snurf—OUCH!" I plummeted . . . and this time it wasn't on purpose . . . at all. What was going on?

Now I was more determined than ever to get it right. I set my sights on another jump and went at it, full steam ahead. "Ready, aim, BLAST OFF!" I shouted and flew like a speeding bullet. I was getting primo-air and ready to try an alley-oop. But just when I was mid-twist, I felt myself losing it. I started **rolling down the windows**—flailing my arms to save the jump, but it was pointless. This fall was even worse, and I **faceplanted** in the snow. **Garage sale**. *Again.*

Just then I heard the scrape-scrape sound of a board stopping behind me. "You're getting some super-sweet air, Snurfette," said a familiar voice. "Want a few tips?"

I turned and looked at the dude standing there in a red jacket and bright yellow hat. "DK!"

He put one finger over his mouth and looked from side to side. "Shh . . . I'm incognito!"

I nodded. Boy, was I embarrassed! The Egg had totally seen my very un-graceful fall. "Been here long?" I asked in a shaky voice.

Donnie Keeler smiled. "Long enough to see that you know what you're doing out here. And long enough to see that you probably just lost your confidence for some reason. But my guess is it'll only take a few **gnarly** jumps to get it all back."

I felt a wave of relief pass over me. "Really?" I asked. "You think I just lost my confidence?"

DK nodded. "Totally. Your form is right-on. But when you're mid-air, it's like something in here"—DK patted his head with his glove—"stops you from doing what's in here." He made a fist and tapped his coat above his heart. "So what's the deal?"

One word flashed in my head . . . and it began with a big fat *K*.

"I think your noggin needs to take a chill pill," DK told me. I knew he was right. I had a gazillion thoughts in my head when I was flying through the air. I wasn't tearing it up the way I was yesterday . . . before the Crazie Kazie dinner, and Jason, and the Snurfer worries and everything else. Too much stuff was clogging my brain!

DK nodded. "Okay, Snurfette, so clear your head. Instead of focusing on the jump, think of something funny. Like what about the waffle mountain? That thing was insane!"

It was big, sure. But funny? Well, not as funny as Marty and Crud putting on a show for everyone outside the diner. Wait a minute.

"I got it!" I exclaimed.

DK gave me a thumbs-up. "Radical! Don't tell me . . . just jump."

I nodded and pulled my goggles snugly over my eyes. The snow blasted from the snowmakers around me, stinging my face with icy flakes. But at that moment, it was just what I needed—a frosty wake-up call, as cold and refreshing as a fruit smoothie. I popped from side-stance to front like a slinky and started weaving toward the giant wall of the pipe.

"Get 'er done, Snurfette!" DK cheered. "You should try an **eggplant**."

Eggplant. I thought of last night's delicious lasagna and pumped my fist into the air. I'd never tried an eggplant before, but I'd seen them done plenty of times. I knew I had the skill to do it . . . I just needed to take a chance. I slid my hand over the little lump in my pocket, and instantly recharged, knowing the BSG charm key ring was safe inside. Then I cleared my mind like DK said and filled it with something funny. That was where the idea came in handy. I pictured Marty on a snowboard cruising down

"I pictured Marty on a snowboard cruising down the slopes with his tiny paws out and ears flying."

the slopes with his tiny paws out and ears flying. Of course, he wore tiny goggles and a tiny jester hat like Dad's with a big pom-pom, along with his blue Snurfer sweater. With this image of Snowboard Marty locked in my head, I went for it.

"You got it, Avery!" DK's voice was a faint echo behind me. I was gathering speed as I slid down again and jumped into a perfect **backside** air.

I rode down to where Donnie was waiting and high-fived him as I slid past. He whistled. "That was star quality, Snurfette. For real!" I couldn't believe it—a real, live Olympic boarder was complimenting my skills.

"Okay, now try a **frontside handplant**," Donnie directed.

"You got it!" I went for it, not hesitating for a second. Wouldn't you know, my frontside handplant was perfect too! DK hollered and whooped. I was flying now and I refused to stop. I shot into the air, snapped my heel edge up, and grabbed it with my front hand—a **melon**. Then I did a sweet **indy**, clutching the toe edge with my back hand. I swished up and down the walls, nailing **roast beefs**, **stalefishes**, **mutes**, and **methods**, executing every trick almost as shred-tastically as Kazie.

After about two hours, my legs were burning but I still wished the fun didn't have to end. Donnie and I weaved our way to the bottom, having a shout-out all the way down. "Whooo-hooo!" I cried.

"Ow-ow-ow!" Donnie hollered.

"Ollie ollie oxen free!" I sang.

Then Donnie flashed by like lightning with a "GERONIMO!"

When we reached the bottom of the pipe, I did some **butterflies**, lifting the front of my board and spinning around in a circle. I felt a little dizzy after, but I could tell DK was impressed. He gave me two thumbs-up as we unclipped and stepped out of our bindings.

"Thanks for everything," I told him.

He waved his hand. "Are you kidding me? A good time was had by all. I'm tired of always competing, you know? It's supposed to be about fun! My dad says that's the number-one rule of sports."

I grinned. "Mine too . . . actually."

DK held out his puffy-gloved fist to tap with mine. "Snurfette, you keep this up, and you'll have nothing to worry about in the Snurfer. You've got it under control."

I nodded but felt a pang of disappointment. I knew what he meant—I'd *have fun* in the Snurfer. Not that I would win. But if I let go of my worries the way I had today, at least I'd leave the Snurfer with a huge smile—the most important thing.

DK looked at his watch and groaned. "Yikes! Now I gotta go meet my coach. Thanks, Snurfette." He gave me a classic DK wink. I was so stunned that he was thanking me that my mouth hung opened as he jogged away. He turned, quickly saluted, and added, "Tell Marty that Crud says hello!" Then he disappeared into the crowd.

Just then I spotted Jason and Dad by the gondola and ran over to meet them. Dad had something in his hand that was covered in wax paper.

"Veggie burger?" Dad offered, holding it up in front of me.

My stomach grumbled before I could even answer, "Yumzer! I could eat four!"

"That's m'girl," Dad said. He looked so proud . . . either of me for my healthy appetite, or of himself for remembering my favorite mountain snack, or maybe both.

"How'd it go, Avery?" Jason asked while I peeled the wrapper off the burger.

"Armmahrgarg," I said. Apparently mouth full of

veggie burger equals impossible to talk, and from the look on Dad's face, it also equals disgusting. I swallowed and tried again. "Amazing!"

I told them all about DK and his awesome advice. Jason and Dad chuckled at the idea of Marty flying through the air on a tiny doggy snowboard.

Later, when we got to Jason's, I hopped out to help him unload his stuff while Dad waited in the car. "Are you glad you tried snowboarding?" I asked him.

"Totally," he said and coughed. "Um, actually I was wondering if—"

"We could go again after the Snurfer?" I finished for him. "Well, duh. Of course! Practice makes perfect, don't you know?"

Jason coughed again. "No, um, I was wondering if you wanted to meet at the Telluride Historical Museum tonight . . . at eight."

I laughed out loud. "Why do you want to go to a boring old museum? Don't you think it'd be more fun to visit Ollie? Ooh, or go *night tubing!*"

"Well, actually," Jason started as he shifted uncomfortably. Oops . . . I hoped I hadn't hurt his feelings! He went on, "The museum is doing their annual storytelling tonight, 'Legends and Lore of Old Colorado.' It's supposed to be pretty cool . . ."

"Oh!" Yikes . . . me and my big mouth! "Yeah, that'd be a lot of fun! I have to ask my dad, but I don't know why he wouldn't go for it." My parents told me to always ask them about plans in private. It was just one of the parent rule thingies. "I'll call you if he says no, but otherwise I'll just see you there, okay?"

Jason gave me the details and then turned to open the door. I bounded out onto the porch, but he called after me. "Hey, Avery?"

"Yeah?" I stopped and spun around to face him.

"I really had a good time today," Jason said slowly, like it was a strange thing for him to be saying, even though it sounded polite enough to me.

"Today rocked," I agreed. "Check you later, gator!" I waved again and ran back to the car.

"So, what do you think, Dad?" I asked after I told him about the storytelling.

"Well, we're going to have dinner at Andie's, but you should be able to make it to the museum at eight. You'll need to invite Kazie, of course."

"Def," I mumbled.

"Def?"

"Definitely," I said in a louder voice, even though *definitely* NOT was what I was thinking. Too bad I didn't really have a choice. I remembered last night's Kazie performance at The Sweet Life. *I'm really not in the mood for a rerun. . . .*

14

Wet Cat

"What?" I asked. I laughed a little nervously. My dad was totally weirding me out with his funny smile.

"Nothing," Dad answered, but he was still smiling. "Did you have a good day?"

"Yup! I'm tired though. But it was worth it. Seriously, Dad, I had a snowboarding lesson with Donnie Keeler. I mean, THE Golden Egg! And"—I stopped so he'd know this part was big—"and, I taught Jason how to snowboard for his first time ever. How cool is *that*?"

Dad nodded. "Very cool. I'm proud of you, Ave."

"Tell me about it!" I said, laughing. I got out of the car and slung my bags over my shoulder. I took some of Dad's stuff too, just to show him that I was growing up and being responsible. I liked Dad knowing I was independent—that I wasn't just the baby of the family anymore. Every step I took I could feel my legs aching, just like they did after an intense soccer game. It was clear—I'd pushed it to the max today.

"Marty! We're hoooome!" I called when we got inside. It was so snug and warm in Dad's house—the best kind of place to come home to after a frosty day on the slopes. In a second Marty scurried into the hallway and leaped up to give me a kiss right on my cheek. "Ha, ha, hey there lil' dude! You miss me today? Aw, I missed you too, M-Dawg!"

Seeing Marty was great, but I couldn't help feeling like something was missing. Of course! I ran upstairs and turned on my computer. I really hoped that at least one of the BSG would be online.

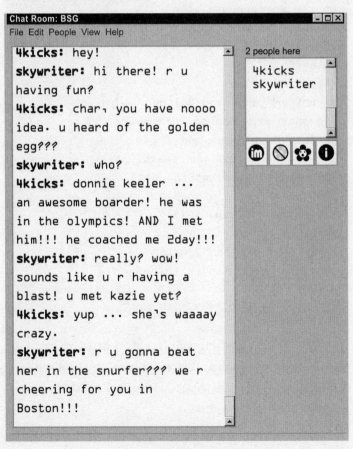

Chat Room: BSG

File Edit People View Help

4kicks: hey!

skywriter: hi there! r u having fun?

4kicks: char, you have noooo idea. u heard of the golden egg???

skywriter: who?

4kicks: donnie keeler ... an awesome boarder! he was in the olympics! AND I met him!!! he coached me 2day!!!

skywriter: really? wow! sounds like u r having a blast! u met kazie yet?

4kicks: yup ... she's waaaay crazy.

skywriter: r u gonna beat her in the snurfer??? we r cheering for you in Boston!!!

2 people here

4kicks
skywriter

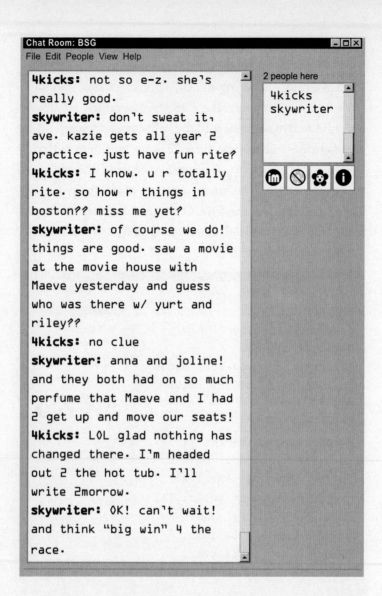

4kicks: not so e-z. she's really good.

skywriter: don't sweat it, ave. kazie gets all year 2 practice. just have fun rite?

4kicks: I know. u r totally rite. so how r things in boston?? miss me yet?

skywriter: of course we do! things are good. saw a movie at the movie house with Maeve yesterday and guess who was there w/ yurt and riley??

4kicks: no clue

skywriter: anna and joline! and they both had on so much perfume that Maeve and I had 2 get up and move our seats!

4kicks: LOL glad nothing has changed there. I'm headed out 2 the hot tub. I'll write 2morrow.

skywriter: OK! can't wait! and think "big win" 4 the race.

2 people here

4kicks
skywriter

I got into my bathing suit, grabbed Maeve's mix CD, and dashed downstairs. This was one of my all-time fave things about Dad's: *the Jacuzzi*. I scooped up Marty on my way out to keep me company.

"No Jacuzzi for you, little guy, but how 'bout a big comfy towel?"

"Arf, arf!" Marty barked back. He was psyched to come outside and hang out with his favorite pal—well, one of his favorites. Dad had fenced in the yard back when he first bought the house to keep the coyotes out. That made it safe for me and our fam . . . including Marty!

When I walked outside I was instantly out-of-control freezing! "Brrrr!" I chattered. Just before I turned into an icicle, I splashed into the steaming hot tub. "Ahhh!" I sighed and closed my eyes.

I tried to relax in the bubbly water and think about absolutely nothing, but all this stuff kept popping into my head. Before this trip I really thought I was a Snurfer contender. AS IF I could actually beat Kazie with just a few days of practice. How could I? In a few more years, she'd probably be an Olympic hopeful herself! I suddenly had the urge to burst out laughing. Me . . . Avery . . . . NOT trying to win a serious sporting event? Hah! "Let's keep this between us, okay, Marty?" I whispered with my eyes still closed.

"Keep what between us?" said a voice.

Startled, I sat up out of the water and felt the icy sting of the cold air hit my face. A long yellow braid twisted around orange ribbons dangled down above me. "Yikes!" I yelled. It was Kazie, and she wasn't alone. A skin-crawling *"Rooooooow, yeooooooow"* told me that right away.

"Scare you? Sorry, dude," she said. But she didn't look sorry . . . not even close.

I wasn't the only scared one. Farkle's second, *"Rooooooow, yeooooooow"* sent Marty scrambling for shelter in my pile of towels underneath the deck chair.

Kazie just laughed. "That is SO funny! Your dog is totally the scaredy-cat! Just look at him."

Marty was huddled underneath a towel. Poor lil' dude, being shoved out of his own place by the monster Franken-cat. "What are you doing here?" I had to ask. Since when was it okay to just *show up* at people's houses with your possessed monster pets? That's what I wanted to know.

"Jake said I could come and use the hot tub anytime." She took off her bathrobe and took two steps back. "Stay here Farkle, my love," she instructed, setting Farkle down on top of the chair Marty was hiding under.

Kazie held her nose and shouted. "One, two, three, CANNONBALL!" She took a running start and launched herself—curled in a ball—into the tub. Water exploded everywhere. It stung my eyes! Kazie was just as bad as her evil Franken-cat.

"RAAAAAAR!" screeched Farkle.

"Yoooow!" howled Marty.

Both of the animals were soaked, and boy, were they mad! Kazie shot out of the water, laughing hysterically. "Oh, man! I got you guys. Sorry, Farkle!"

Marty was cowering away from one very, very grouchy Maine coon. "I'm outta here," I said. I slipped out of the hot tub, shivering like crazy, and wrapped myself in a towel.

"C'mon, Avery. I was just trying to have a little fun. Don't be a baby."

Have a little fun? Don't be a baby? Now she'd really gone too far! "You know what?" I began.

Kazie was back-floating in the tub . . . happy as a clam. She bent her head back and blew bubbles out of her nose. "What?" she asked.

I was about to tell her that Avery Koh Madden was no baby and THE QUEEN of fun. *Wait a minute,* I thought. What's more babyish than lecturing someone that you're fun? Kazie had trapped me. How'd she do that? "Never mind!" I snapped.

I grabbed up Marty and wrapped him in a towel. Without saying a word to Kazie, I sloshed into the house, leaving a trail of icy puddles. What was it about that girl that always bugged me? Back at school I could tell anybody anything, no prob. Kazie seemed to have a special talent for always making me look and feel like someone's dorky baby sister.

I went upstairs to get showered and dressed. I tried my hardest to shampoo away my frustration with Kazie. I mean, everyone could be a little annoying sometimes, right? I knew I could be. I turned off the water and actually felt a little better. Kazie was just messing around. No big deal.

When I opened the bathroom door, Marty was waiting right outside, curled up on a towel he'd dragged over. He was staying close to me, and far, far away from freaky Farkle. Even smarty-pants pooches like Marty knew their limits. I wrapped Marty in my warm fleece blanket and gave him a hug. "It's okay, lil' guy," I assured him. "Farkle's a creepy, mean, mean cat. Just stick to fun, sweet Border Jacks like Crud and your posse at home. Remember Louie, La Fanny, Bella, and the rest of your pals? They think you're the man." I scratched Marty behind his little ears.

I threw on my jeans and my favorite blue ATS hoodie. Unfortunately, I noticed something not-so-good in the window's reflection. *Oops*. The shoulder was still stained with tomato sauce . . . remains of a little food fight I had with Scott. If I showed up in tomato sauce, Kazie would find some way to tease me about it, and I'd be so annoyed.

I chose a red sweater that Katani helped me pick out a few weeks before. She had all these special reasons for why the color of it was supposed to be just right for me or something, but I wasn't paying too much attention. Now I could see, though, that Kgirl was totally right-on. I was still comfy, but I also looked good. *Sweeeeet!* I thought. *Thanks, Kgirl!*

It was darker now. I peeked outside to check out the hot tub below and sure enough, Kazie had finally gone home. "Yessssss!" I slapped Marty a paw-five, and I swear, if dogs really did smile, Marty was grinning from ear to ear now that there was no sign of the Farkelator.

Downstairs, Dad was in the kitchen shaking out a bag of my ultimate favorite Telluride Organic Spicy Chips into a bowl on the table. Not only that, next to the bowl were two plates, and on top of those plates were two awesomely delish-looking turkey subs. My mouth watered instantly.

Dad looked nice. Really nice. He was wearing a brown sweater with a brown matching jacket. Wait a minute, weren't we going to Andie's for dinner? I looked at Dad, then at the sandwiches, then back at Dad.

"Okay, Dad, spill it. What's going on?"

"Well, the truth is, Avery . . ." he leaned over the counter and looked slyly from side to side. Then he said in a quiet voice, "Andie's a terrible cook."

I covered my mouth with my hand. "No way!"

"Way." Dad put a finger over his mouth and pointed to the door of the downstairs bathroom. I could hear the shower running. "Kazie's in there," he explained, then went on extra-quietly, "so we've got to eat up fast."

"Why doesn't Kazie just use her own shower?" I grumbled, looking around for the Farkle-monster.

Dad pushed a plate over to me. "Be nice, Avery," he cautioned. "There's plenty of water to go around."

I sighed and sank my teeth into a mustard-covered sandwich. I had to give Dad credit—it really hit the spot. "So . . . Dad . . . I want to know more about Andie being a lousy cook."

Dad raised his eyebrows. "Hey, don't get me wrong. Andie's an unbelievable store manager, she's an excellent mother, an independent woman, and, most importantly, a really great friend. But when it comes to cooking . . ." Dad made a grossed-out face that was so funny I really had to cover my mouth—to NOT laugh out loud.

"Like Mom," I noted. Mom wasn't a great cook either . . . which is why we usually ordered out.

"Exactly," said Dad. We concentrated on our sandwiches for a while without talking. I thought about what Dad said. He'd never had a real girlfriend before— not since I'd been alive, anyway. Andie must have been someone he liked. A lot. It made me wonder . . .

"Dad, I know I asked you this before but . . ." I stopped

and looked at him. I was serious now. I wanted him to know it. "Do you think you might marry Andie . . . someday?"

Silence. Ugh. I *hated* silences like that. "It's impossible for me to answer that question now, Avery. I really care about Andie, but—"

"Okay, Snurfman!" Kazie called from the hallway. "I'm ready to go! Let's get this show on the road."

Not now! I wanted to scream.

Dad grabbed the plates and dropped them into the sink. It made me feel kind of good that we had this little secret dinner, just the two of us. "We'll finish talking about the, um, Snurfer later, Ave," Dad said as Kazie burst into the kitchen holding a hissing beastie thing in her arms.

The Snurfer. I wished he'd said anything but that. When Kazie heard the word Snurfer, she made this happy/goofy face, like she was so sure she had the whole competition in her pocket. "Hi, guys. You talking about the Snurfer?"

How come she was so calm and friendly? Didn't she get that she was just really rude to me outside? Half of me felt dizzy and the other half felt like flicking a potato chip at Kazie's head. Ugh. I didn't do either, though. I just grabbed my coat and followed Dad and Kazie out the door.

CHAPTER
15

Stalefish Air

H ello! Welcome!" Andie opened the door to her little red house on the other side of town. Kazie whooshed by her mom and Farkle bounded by too. "Boots, Kazie!" Andie reminded her. Kazie groaned and stopped to take off her wet, snowy shoes.

The walls inside the Walkers' house were painted bright yellow. There was artwork everywhere, paintings that looked like someone had blasted paintballs on a canvas, I thought, and lots of bronze sculptures of horses and cowboys. It was like a mini-museum, but cooler because everything was so colorful. Navajo rugs covered the floor, and the lamps were made from stumps of trees that had been coated in gloss—totally western style! A fire crackled in the fireplace. Dad's house had the cozy thing going for it, but Andie's was plain-old cool! I think I'd feel happy 24/7 if I lived in such a fun, bright place.

Andie looked all dressed-up tonight. She was wearing a white blouse with a long, dark green skirt. Her silky-straight hair was tucked behind dangly silver earrings. *Welcome to the world of grown-up dates!* I thought. She gave me a hug and kissed my cheek in that weird adult way. Then she kissed Dad too but not on the cheek. For some reason I glanced at Kazie at that instant and saw her make a *blech* face. I realized that I was making one too! We both cracked up.

"What are you two giggling at?" Dad asked. He gave me a noogie on my head.

"Ouch! I surrender, I surrender!" I laughed.

"All right." Andie's cheeks were pink. "Let's get this party started. Can I get you something to drink, Avery? I've got cranberry juice, fruit punch, iced tea . . ."

Whoa. She'd remembered that I didn't drink soda. That was pretty nice. Usually parents forgot about that one right away. "Cranberry juice, please," I replied.

"Can I have a root beer float, Mom? Pleeeease? Jake made me one last time!" Kazie begged.

"It's true," Dad said. His eyes sparkled with mischief. "Can I have one too?"

Andie threw up her arms but smiled anyway. "What in ze vorld am I going to do viff you?" she said in her funny fake accent. "Root beer floats et iz."

Kazie looked me up and down. "Come on," she finally offered. "I'll show you my place."

I realized pretty soon that Kazie wasn't kidding when she said *her* place. As we walked through the den, dining room, and kitchen, one thing was obvious: The whole place was like a Crazie Kazie shrine. And when it came to the Kazie Fan Club, the president was none other than

Andie Walker herself. Maybe it was because Kazie was all Andie had, I mean, without a husband or any other kids or anything. There was Farkle too, I guess, but come on. I'd rather put up photos of Bigfoot in my living room than of that Franken-cat McEvil!

Kazie's baby pictures cluttered the tables, and boarding trophies were randomly stuck on different shelves. It reminded me a little of Charlotte's house, and how her dad kept tons of pictures of her around. Except Kazie was the polar opposite of Charlotte . . . in more ways than one.

I wondered what it was like for Char and Kazie, only having one parent. I felt pretty lucky that I had two people to turn to. Even though Dad was far away most of the time, he was always there for me on the phone to make me laugh if I had a bad day or talk me through a sticky situation. I remembered once when Dad took a red-eye flight at three a.m. all the way from Telluride just to get to Boston in time to see my soccer tournament on Saturday morning. He'd been my biggest fan that day too. He cheered so loud that all the kids kept looking up in the stands to see what the racket was all about. I figured Kazie and I were both lucky that our parents thought we were totally awesome.

Kazie told me about how Andie was a total art nut and how all the pieces of artwork were gifts from her friends who she went to art school with. "Mom's into photography too," Kazie explained. "Which is why . . ." she used her hands to frame her head and smiled like she was in a picture.

"Picture overload!" I exclaimed.

Kazie laughed. "Exactly."

As we walked back into the kitchen, a strange (and scary) odor hit me right away.

"So I gotta warn you," Kazie began, "My mom's not exactly the greatest cook in the world."

"Oh, yeah?" I choked out. I had to choke it out because the smell coming from the kitchen stove was so weird I was trying not to breathe through my nose. "What did she make for dinner?" I asked, my voice sounding like Kermit the Frog on account of my no-nose-breathing rule.

Kazie fanned her face and shook her head. "It's too gross to say. Honestly, I'd tell you, but I'm afraid you'd run away right now. I told Mom to order Chinese food or something, but noooooo, she wanted to do a 'home-cooked meal.' News flash: We're in deep trouble!"

I shivered. That horrible smell made me think that Kazie knew what she was talking about.

"Jake's an awesome cook though, huh?" Kazie said.

"Who's an awesome cook?" asked Andie. She and Dad walked into the kitchen, and I couldn't help but feel a little bad when I saw the huge smile on Andie's face.

"Um, my brother, Scott," I answered quickly.

"*Nice save!*" Kazie mouthed. She even walked behind me and slapped me five! Weird . . . was she being really, truly nice to me, or was it my imagination? I couldn't keep up with Crazie Kazie's program.

Pretty soon it was time to sit down to dinner. While Andie was in the kitchen slamming cabinet doors and banging pots and pans, Kazie was in the dining room trying to convince Dad and me to make a run for it. "I'm serious, guys. If we leave now, we might make it."

"Kazie . . ." Dad warned, but I could tell he was definitely laughing on the inside.

"Think about it, Jake! The Snurfmobile can be our getaway car. And Farkle can be our attack cat! It would totally work. Pleeeeaase?"

At that moment, Andie used her back to push open the kitchen door. She didn't look as clean and put-together anymore. There was a streak of flour smudged across her forehead and her white blouse looked kind of like one of those abstract splatter paintings that was hanging in the front hall. Andie was holding something with pot holders in her hands. "I hope you brought your appetites!" she said proudly and plunked the dish in the middle of the table.

"Oh, Andie, this looks fabulous!" Dad gushed.

I felt someone kick me underneath the table. *"Liar!"* Kazie coughed, pretending to clear her throat.

Luckily, Andie hadn't noticed. "Well, I remembered that Avery isn't crazy about red meat, so I made my mother's famous tuna noodle casserole."

At the same time the three of us—Dad, Kazie, and I—all leaned in to see what the food was that we were supposed to eat. Inside a white rectangular dish was the single most disgusting thing I'd ever laid eyes on . . . as far as food goes. It was like a combination of every leftover on the face of the planet. The only parts I recognized were macaroni and cheese, peas, and tuna fish chunks. I guess those things alone wouldn't have been too bad, but together? And to make matters worse, there were these random splotches of mayo floating in it. The little noodles at the top were brown, rock-solid burned crusties and . . . could it be? Were the peas still *frozen*?

Kazie must have been thinking the same thing, because she used her spoon to scoop up a little blob, picked out a single green pea, and ate it. "Oh, man! Mom, this pea's still cold!"

Andie turned beet red and laughed nervously. "Heh-heh, well I forgot to add the peas until five minutes ago. Maybe they haven't fully defrosted yet. I'd put it all back in the oven but . . ." The obvious "but" was the fact that the noodles were the color of coffee grounds and practically fossilized after their stay in Andie's oven.

Dad gave a big "AHEM," and grabbed the serving spoon. "Who wants first dibs?" When no one spoke, he said, "Avery?" I reluctantly handed my plate over while my stomach flopped around. I was afraid to even look at the food in front of me . . . let alone *digest* it.

But maybe I was in luck. Dad was chipping away at the top layer of the casserole and still hadn't been able to break the hard noodle shield. "Ugh, ugh!" he grunted as he tried to shove the spoon into a block of cheese. "Should we try a knife?"

Andie shook her head and looked up at my dad, her face full of worry. "No, Jake . . . it's supposed to slide right in." She just seemed confused—like she didn't know *why* the casserole wasn't working! Oh, man. . . .

Suddenly Kazie sniffed the air. "Hey, do you guys smell that? Is something burning?"

"MY BISCUITS!" Andie leaped up. Kazie banged her head down on her empty plate.

A minute later Andie returned with a basket of tiny black-and-brown dough balls. She placed them on the table next to the casserole and sat down again, looking upset with herself. Dad reached over and rubbed her back. "They might be a wee bit on the well-done side," he said in a soft voice.

Without a word Kazie stuck her hand into the basket, pulled out a little burned-up biscuit, and chucked it on the ground. It rolled with the speed of a baseball, straight under the legs of a cowboy statue in the other room. "Score!" Kazie cried. "Hole in one!"

Dad made a laugh-snort and covered his mouth. Then I had to cough to cover up mine. That did it. Andie burst out giggling. Soon we were all hysterical at the idea of actually eating a bite of the food that Andie had made.

"It's pretty bad, isn't it?" she asked, dabbing her eyes from laughing so hard.

"I gotta tell you, Mom," Kazie said. "It ain't good."

"Well, you know what they say," Dad said, winking at me. "It's never too late . . . for pizza. This one's on me." He took out his cell phone and dialed the number for The Brown Dog Pizzeria.

"You want to see my room?" Kazie asked while we waited for the pizza.

"Sure." I was a little surprised but happy, too. Pizza was coming and things were looking up!

I followed Kazie upstairs, where she hadn't taken me during the earlier tour. Now she seemed pretty excited to show off her stuff.

"Whoa!" I exclaimed once the door to her bedroom opened. Kazie's walls were covered with posters and magazine cutouts—and they weren't snowboarding pictures. They were animals! *Kazie is an animal nut like me,*

I thought. There were tigers on the ceiling, walruses taped to the closet, crocodiles over her bureau, and a moose on her door. And, she had the little critters too, like cats, dogs, hamsters, bunnies, you know . . . the pet crew.

The real-live animal (that would be Farkle . . . Marty's nemesis) was lying on Kazie's bed, fast asleep. Kazie saw me looking at Farkle and laughed a little. "I know he's kinda crabby."

My mouth hung open. "Kinda?"

Kazie sat in her desk chair and spun herself around. "Well, it's not totally his fault. He's a stray, you know? I found him wandering alone by a river back when we lived in New Hampshire. Farkle was just a kitten and he was all wet and dirty. I knew his mom was long gone. So I took him in and took care of him. He's always been grouchy with other people, but I kinda think it's because he didn't have anyone when he was a baby. He only trusts me."

I guess it made sense. Sure, Farkle seemed scary (and evil), but it'd be hard if you were just a little kitty left alone to find your way in the wild. Kazie was pretty cool to give a cat like that a lot of love.

"Marty's a stray too," I told her.

Kazie tilted her head and smiled. "No way! He's so sweet though."

"I know, well, that's Marty for you. My friends and I found him in a garbage can. He was wicked dirty, but after we bathed him and he was so cute, we all wanted to keep him. But we put up posters and stuff to try to find the owners, just in case."

"And no one answered?" Kazie seemed fascinated.

"Nope!"

Kazie got out of her chair and snuggled on her bed next to Farkle. She was way into my Marty story and still waiting for me to keep talking. "So how'd *you* get to be the one to keep him?" she asked.

"Ugh, I didn't," I admitted with a shrug. "My mom's allergic to dogs, so Marty usually lives with my friend Charlotte. But we all take care of him."

"Errrr!" Kazie pretended to be aggravated for me. I laughed. Was I actually starting to like this girl? "I'd be so bummed if my Farkly-Warkly had to live with, like, Tessa or Siobhan or something! How do you stand it?"

I glanced at a rainforest poster above Kazie's bed and knew my next piece of news would be pretty impressive. "Actually, I've got other pets too. Frogster. He's a—"

"Lemme guess," Kazie interrupted. "A panda?" Her mouth cracked into a smile.

"And I got Walter, and he's a . . ." I paused to let Kazie guess this one.

"No clue!" she said.

"Snake," I declared proudly.

"Whoa, dude! Your mom let you have a snake? That's off the hook! I always wanted to have a snake."

"Did Andie say no?" I asked.

"I said no!" She pointed at the furry feline snoozing on the bed beside her. "I didn't trust that guy." We both laughed at this. Think about it! A cat that's scarier than a snake . . . yikes!

Just then we heard the door creak open downstairs. Kazie sat upright and wrinkled her nose, purposely acting like a dog on the scent. *Sniff, sniff. Sniff, sniff.* "I smell . . . cheese . . . tomato sauce . . ."

"GIRLS! DINNER!" Dad hollered.

"Yes!" we exclaimed at the same time. We dashed out of the room and pounded down the stairs to the warm box of pizza waiting for us in the kitchen. This was dinner number two for me, but I had plenty of room after all my hardcore boarding.

Kazie and I dove for the two biggest slices, drenched with cheese and covered with mushrooms and grilled barbecue chicken. Andie took a piece next and smiled after her first gigantic bite.

"Mmm! Now *this* is what I call dinner!" Dad looked happy and put his arm around Andie's shoulders. I could see why he liked her. Besides trying to make sure that I had food to eat, she was even chill about her cooking disaster. Andie was a really great sport.

Dad suddenly tapped his watch. "Hey, Avery. It's seven forty-five—better get a move on."

"Oh, man! I gotta go!" I wasn't sure what to do first—grab my coat or shove the pizza into my mouth in one huge bite!

"Go where?" Kazie asked.

Oops! I'd promised Dad that I'd invite her. He raised an eyebrow at me. Before I'd been dreading it, but Kazie and I were suddenly having so much fun that it completely slipped my mind. "I'm going to the museum tonight to a storytelling thing. Wanna come?"

"Legends and Lore? That's tonight? Mom . . ." Kazie looked at Andie. "Can I?"

Andie glanced at Dad and I saw them smile at each other. "I don't see why not," she said.

"Yesssss!" Kazie bolted out of the room and when she came back she had both of our coats. "Let's take our pizza on the road, Avery."

That was fine with me. Kazie moved like a tornado. She ran to the counter, got paper towels, and on her way back to the pizza managed to high-five Dad and give her mom a kiss good-bye. I felt dizzy just watching her. My eyeballs were bouncing back and forth!

"Sweeeeet dude! Let's rock!" Kazie galloped out the front door.

"Bye, Dad!" I called. "See ya later, Andie."

Dad grabbed my hood as I was running so for a second there I was like the Roadrunner. My legs were going but I wasn't moving an inch! "Just one second, young lady," Dad said.

"Aw, what now, Dad?"

He slipped his digital camera into my hand. "Take some pictures of you and Kazie tonight, okay? Remember, I can never get enough!"

I rolled my eyes but slipped the camera in my pocket. "Byeeee!" I sang and ran out the door.

On the way to the museum, Kazie and I had energy to spare. We jogged all the way to the end of the block. Kazie stopped, panting, and pointed up to the ski resort, where the trails were shimmering like white ribbons. "See that thick one up there?" she said. "That's the pipe. Doesn't it look so cool at night?"

The pipe was the thickest of the lit-up trails. Kazie was

right. Its light was almost a gold color. My heart beat faster just looking at it. That's what happened when you truly loved boarding, I thought.

"I can't *wait* for the Snurfer," Kazie declared. "Aren't you sooo excited?"

She seemed to have forgotten our awkward moment on the mountain earlier that day. Or maybe with Kazie it was all kind of a joke—all competition. "I'm pretty pumped," I said carefully.

Kazie started walking again, like she was in a daze. "It's going to be so off the hook, dude. Do you know how many TV stations are going to be covering this? Siobhan said that ESPN might even be there! If my first-place victory makes it onto ESPN, coaches all over the country will want me. I'm telling you, Avery . . . I'd be set." She turned to me with wide eyes.

My stomach flopped a little, and I wasn't sure how to respond. What did she expect me to do, root for her to win? I was glad that we were kind of starting to be friends, but it was still pretty annoying that she totally dismissed my boarding skills. But then, she hadn't really seen what I could do, and was it even a good idea to be making friends with my biggest competitor? I didn't really know what to think.

16

Rodeo Flip

K azie and I turned the corner to the museum and almost walked smack into Tessa and Siobhan. "Kazie! We were looking for you!" Tessa laughed. They looped their arms over Kazie's shoulders so she was in the middle of them both. I stood there waiting, wondering if anyone was going to bother with a "Hey, Avery," or something. Nope! I automatically reached into my pocket and felt around for the charm key ring and pen from Charlotte. Still there. Phew. I suddenly missed my friends more than ever.

"Hey, guys," said Kazie. "We're headed to the museum for the storytelling thing. What's up?"

"The whole crew's going night sledding in Town Park," Siobhan told Kazie. "And you are totally coming." The girls started to walk Kazie away in the other direction, but Kazie managed to wiggle herself away.

"Hold on, hold on," Kazie commanded. She took a deep breath and looked at me. "My mom thinks I'm going to this storytelling thing with *her*." She nodded in my direction.

I felt my cheeks burn. So that's how it was going to be! One second we were friends and the next I was "her" — just an unimportant ant that was getting in the way of her hanging out with the crew.

"So just call your mom and tell her there's been a change of plans," Siobhan suggested.

Kazie grinned. "Yeah . . . okay!" She began to dial the numbers. "You in?" she asked me.

I shook my head. "No, thanks," I told her. "I'm meeting Jason at the museum." Kazie's eyebrows lifted. Tessa looked like she'd gotten the wind knocked out of her. Oops. I guess I hadn't explained that part of the plan to Kazie back at the house.

"*You're* meeting Jason?" Tessa gaped. "Is it, like, a date?"

I rolled my eyes. What was up with these kids always thinking that just because you hang out with a guy friend it means you're out on a date? Hello! "Date" and "Avery" were two words that had never—in the history of my life—been used in the same sentence. Wait till I told the BSG about this one. "Date? Um, no. Definitely not. We're just friends, guys. Seriously."

Tessa turned up her nose and sniffed in a know-it-all voice. "Okay, I believe you." She turned to Siobhan and Kazie and explained, "We already know that Jason's really not the dating type. Obviously." She tossed her stick-straight red hair over her shoulder. "Right, Kazie, *right?*"

Kazie was on the phone with Andie. She covered the

receiver. "Come on, dude. Don't worry about Jason. He and Avery *are* friends."

I almost died. One second ago I was an ant, and now Kazie was defending me? I couldn't nail this girl down! One second she could be so annoying and the next she was sweet as pie.

"Okay, Mom. Yup. I will." She flipped down the phone. "Avery, are you cool with me going?" she asked.

I could see the museum a block ahead. "Totally," I told her. "Catch you later."

Then Kazie did something way unexpected. She put her fist out to do the weird, complicated secret handshake that I'd seen her do with Dad . . . *with me*. Kazie didn't say a word—just made the motions and I followed her lead. "Later, dude," she said and turned to cross the street.

"Bye, Avery!" called Siobhan as they went away.

"Hmph!" Tessa snorted. She was still mad about me hanging out with Jason, but I didn't care at all. Kazie turned around once and gave me a thumbs-up and a wave. I guess we were starting to be friends after all.

I ran the rest of the way to the museum and pulled open the heavy green door. A blast of warm air surrounded me as I stepped inside. There were people everywhere—kids, parents, babies—all headed in different directions. Some were trying to snag a cookie and hot chocolate and others were in a line for the bathroom that wrapped around the whole wall. I craned my neck to see where Jason was but I couldn't find him. That was the thing about being short— not so handy in crowds. I reached into my pocket and gave the BSG pen key ring a squeeze. It made me feel a little better, a little braver, and seemed to always give me good luck.

Then I noticed a small girl standing near the staircase. It was dark in her corner, sort of underneath the stairwell. She was dressed up like she could've been plucked right out of an old western movie. Her dress was pink with puffy sleeves and an apron. She even wore a bonnet. She looked very pale. Since she was the only person not talking to anyone, I thought maybe she could give me directions to the storytelling.

"Excuse me," I said. She stared up at me with big, empty eyes. She wasn't smiling. "Excuse me," I repeated. "How do I get to Legends and Lore?"

She lifted a finger—almost in slow motion—and pointed up the stairs.

"Cool!" I said and bolted past her. I suddenly remembered my manners (which I tended to forget) and turned around to say thanks. But when I did, there was absolutely no sign of her. *Weird, I wonder where she went.* The hairs on the back of my neck stood up a little. I was definitely creeped out, and it reminded of the feeling I got from the spooky ghost town in Montana I'd visited with the BSG.

At the top of the stairs, I wasn't sure which way to go again. I must have looked pretty lost because a tall girl around my age with long, red hair and striking blue eyes walked over to me. (Maeve would have loved to meet this girl!) "You looking for Legends and Lore?" she asked with a friendly smile. I nodded, and she pointed toward a big door. "It's in there. I come to Legends and Lore every time

I visit Telluride. Is this your first time?"

"Yep," I told her. "Most of the year I live in Boston with my mom, but I'm visiting my dad right now."

"I'm from out of town too—Charlevoix, Michigan," she told me. "And I'm Grace, by the way."

"Avery," I informed her, introducing myself. "Gotta run—see you in there!"

She seems really nice, I thought as I hurried into the auditorium, looking around for Jason. Hopefully he was here and didn't forget about the whole thing. I mean, I hadn't talked to him since we dropped him off earlier. Suddenly, I spotted him up near the front row. Frankie was there too, standing on a chair right beside him. His crazy brown hair was sticking straight up.

Jason waved until I waved back and hurried over. "I'm glad you found me!" Jason said. "I was going to meet you downstairs, but it started filling up fast! I didn't want to risk not getting a good seat."

"Good call!" I agreed. "Hey, did you notice that girl by the stairs?"

"Jason! Jason!" Frankie bonked Jason on the head.

"Hold on a sec, Frankie. Wait, notice what girl, Avery? I didn't see any girl . . ."

Ick. Now I was really getting the heebie-jeebies. "Okay, well, downstairs there was this . . . this . . . girl who seemed like she was old-fashioned, and she was in this dress, right, but she was afraid to talk to me, I think, and well, she disappeared just after, and maybe she was a . . . a . . ."

Jason nodded at me to continue. I gulped. "A ghost?" Jason just started to chuckle. "Come on. What?" I asked.

"That's an actress, Avery. They have a couple of kids dress up just to get everyone in the moooooood." He intoned "mood" in a low, trembling voice and wiggled his fingers in the air. "And I did see her."

I jokingly pattered my fists against his arm.

"Ha, ha! Got you!" He started laughing. Frankie did too, even though I seriously doubt Frankie knew what he was laughing at, besides me. He hammered Jason's head again. "Jason, Jason," he yammered. "Is Avery a baby? Is she 'fraid?"

"Yup," Jason said. "Avery's afraid of the scaaaary museum ghosts!"

"Oh, yeah?" I asked. I knew exactly how to give Jason a taste of his own medicine. I took the camera out of my pocket and said, "Say FLEAS!"

Now Jason looked like *he'd* seen a ghost! But instead of smiling he lifted Frankie up, held the little kid in front of his head, and cried, "No! Don't shoot!"

But it was too late. I captured a very funny picture—of Frankie sitting on Jason's shoulder laughing hysterically.

"Don't worry. I'll get my revenge," I promised slyly. But it would have to wait until later, because right at that moment a man walked onto the small stage at the front of the room.

He looked a little older than Dad. Underneath his cowboy hat I could see gray hairs peeking out. He wore jeans and a leather jacket with long fringe on the sleeves and bottom. On his feet were shiny cowboy boots.

The room got quiet in a second . . . so quiet you could've

heard a ghost whisper. Even Frankie stopped poking Jason and finally sat down without a word.

"Howdy. Good evening, ladies and gents." He tipped his hat and sat down in a wooden rocking chair in the middle of the stage. "My name is Cowboy Jack, and I'm mighty pleased that y'all took time out of yer night to come and hear one of my stories."

The room grew dark. The only trickle of light was on Cowboy Jack's face.

"Boo!" Jason whispered in my ear and I nearly jumped right out of my seat. "Remember . . . no such thing as ghosts."

I fake glared. "Hey, watch it with that 'boo' business!"

Faint banjo music started playing from the speakers as Cowboy Jack began his story.

"Tonight I'd like to tell y'all about an old friend of mine who was a legendary outlaw around these parts. Now, I know what yer probably thinking about my friend. Yer thinkin' he was some crazy criminal or a hot-headed, son-of-a-gun who'd be yer best friend one second . . . and yer worst enemy the next. And guess what? You'd be right, except for one thing. This outlaw . . . was a she.

"Candy McDougal was her name. She was the oldest of seven kids on a farm outside of Denver. Times were tough. You see, her daddy was a gambler and he got into some pretty bad scrapes when he'd go into the city. One night, he gambled away two of the family's horses. The next time, it was the farm. Her momma was so fed up she up and left that man. She gathered up

Candy and her brothers and sisters and they left in the middle of the night.

"But there was a problem. Candy was sixteen and in love. She had pledged her undying devotion to a boy named Johnny who was a poor schoolteacher in Denver. Candy's momma made it as far as Salt Lake City when Candy ran away, trying to run herself back east to Denver to the man she loved.

"Now, the West was no place to be running around alone . . . especially if you was sixteen years old. Candy figured out soon that she needed money for food and a place to sleep. That's when she met up with Kyle Larimer and the Red Mountain Gang. Larimer and his gang was bank robbers, trying to bust up every bank west of the Mississippi. People all over knew the Red Mountain Gang by the red feathers they wore in their cowboy hats. Larimer said Candy could hitch along with them, provided she did all the cooking and cleaning and mending of their clothes. Candy agreed and that was that. The thing was, Larimer, well, he wasn't exactly the best shot. And he wasn't exactly the bravest man, neither. Whenever something got fouled up in one of his robbing operations, him and the gang was always chased out of town and his men was always getting themselves shot or worse.

"One day, Candy decided that she'd had enough of the cookin' and washin' and sewin'. She was anxious to build up her little nest egg and get back on the road to Denver. Seein' where the real money was comin' from in this operation, Candy took matters into her own hands. She'd become quite handy with a needle during her months with the Red Mountain Gang and she sewed herself a get-up that was identical to the one that Larimer wore . . . right down to the red feather in the hat. She took off early one morning and rode on into town. And I'll tell you, Candy went and robbed a bank clean like she'd been doin' it all her life! She rode back up to the Red Mountain Gang's camp with a trunk full of gold. From that day on, she and Larimer were partners. All people were talking about was Kyle Larimer and his mysterious bank-robbing buddy. What nobody knew'd was that his partner was a girl! A sixteen-year-old girl at that.

"Well, the gang eventually made it back to Denver, and Candy knew it was time to say her good-byes. But Larimer wouldn't let her go. Some people thought he was in love with her. Some people just thought he needed her too much. Don't matter none. He said if she ever left him, she'd be sorry. So like her momma, Candy made up her mind to run away in the middle of the night. She took her share of the gold and got on a horse and rode. But if there was one thing that ol' Larimer was good at, it was ridin'. He was on her trail within the hour, and followed her all the way up the mountains to the pass right outside of Denver. Thing is, half the people in Denver heard Larimer whooping and hollering so loud, they was calling for the sheriff. Authorities was waiting for Larimer and his partner to ride on through.

"Now, let me tell y'all—Candy wasn't stupid. She knew'd what they was all expecting: some hardened criminal with a handlebar mustache. So right before she rode on through, she leaped off her horse and changed back into her dress, and rode sidesaddle into the city so everyone done know'd she was a lady. They caught Larimer all right. Caught him red-handed, waving his pistol in the air. But Candy, well, no one ever found her. Some say she changed her name and married that teacher. Some say ol' Larimer caught up with her when he got out of jail and followed through on his word. But one thing's for sure: the Legend of Candy McDougal is one of the greatest mysteries around. And she was one tough cookie."

I'd been so lost in the story, I forgot that Cowboy Jack was even talking until the audience started clapping. The lights turned on and Jack stood up to take a bow. Frankie got wiggly as soon as Jack stopped talking. "Jason, can we go now?" he whined.

"Sure, buddy," Jason said, then he turned to me. "You want to come home with us, Avery? It's only eight thirty. I'm going to give Ollie a flying lesson tonight."

"Yeah! I'm in!" I answered quickly. I ignored Frankie's whimpering noises. I was used to them by now. Then I remembered my big mistake last time I went to Jason's house and added, "I just have to call my dad and make sure it's okay."

I fished around in my pocket for some change and ran outside to use the pay phone in the lobby. "Watch my stuff," I told Jason on the way.

Getting permission from Dad was a cinch. He was

really happy that I'd learned my lesson from the other night and called. "I'll pick you up at ten," he said. "And have fun." Well that was a no-brainer. It seemed like Jason and I had fun no matter what—even snowboarding when he'd never ever done it before, and that said something!

Cowboy Jack was leaving through the side door just as I was coming back in. "Hey, thanks for the awesome story!" I told him.

He tipped his hat and looked at the floor. "Why, thank you, little lady."

Little lady! That cracked me up. "How did you learn the stories?" I asked.

Jack shrugged. "Dunno. They're legends. You hear them a couple of times and retell them and then the legend continues. But 'The Legend of Candy McDougal' has always been my favorite."

"Oh, yeah? Why?"

Jack motioned me closer with his finger and said something in a voice that was so quiet I wasn't even sure if I heard it right or if I was just imagining it. But I think he said: "I'm Johnny!" He put his finger over his lips and walked away without another word.

17

Roast Beef Air

When we got back to the Hulberts' house, someone opened the door before Jason even touched the doorknob. A policeman stood there in his uniform, smiling at all three of us.

"Dad!" Frankie threw his arms around the officer's legs.

"Hi, Fred," Jason said. "Avery, this is my foster dad, Fred. Fred, *this* is Avery."

Fred gave me a big, strong handshake. "Pleasure to meet you, Avery. Jason's told us so many wonderful things about you."

"Thanks," I answered, feeling my mouth creep into a little smile.

"Yeah, okay, Fred. *Thanks,*" Jason muttered and led the way into the house.

Inside it was warm and smelled like chocolate— chocolate cake, to be exact. "Bonnie's been baking," Fred announced to us. "She wanted you guys to have something sweet for after the stories. And let me tell you, you're in for a treat! Bonnie's the best baker in the entire world, in my humble opinion."

Bonnie pointed her wooden spoon at Fred. "Now, you stop that!" she ordered, in a voice that meant she really didn't want him to stop that at all. Jason looked like he could just about die on the spot. As for me, I couldn't *wait* to have a piece of homemade chocolate cake. Bonnie's hot chocolate was so fantabulous, I figured her cake would be out of control. What did Dad call it? Nirvana!

And guess what? I was right.

We all sat down and got a big piece of what Bonnie called her famous "Better Than Your Momma's Chocolate Cake." There were three layers. The top was a moist chocolate cake, the middle was a fluffy chocolate mousse cake, and the bottom was a rich, thick chocolate torte. Sugary, homemade fudge frosting separated the layers and smothered the outside. Most of the cake went right into my stomach, but some of it was chilling out on my face. I learned this factoid from Fred.

"Jason, your friend has grown the most impressive goatee . . . and it only took as long as dessert!" A goatee was a little tuft of a beard, right on the chin. Dad tried to grow a goatee one summer, but my brothers and I took one look at his stubbly chin and said, "Absolutely not, dude!"

I laughed and wiped my face right away. "It's a delicious goatee," I told Bonnie.

"Why, thank you very much."

"Yum in my tummy!" Frankie declared. "Jason, will you play checkers with me?"

Now if I were Jason, I probably would've said, "Do I have to?"

But Jason just smiled at Frankie. I think he was going to say okay, but Fred spoke up first. "I'll play checkers with you, buddy. Jason's got company right now."

Frankie grumbled. "Fine." But he honestly looked at me like he wanted me to melt into slime on the floor. I wanted to get away from that table and FAST.

"Jason, why don't you and Avery go down to the basement to check on Radley?" Bonnie suggested. Wow, first the chocolate cake and now a clever getaway plan! That woman deserves a medal, I thought.

We took our plates over to the counter and headed downstairs. I was pretty psyched about seeing Radley again. The feeling was mutual. As soon as Radley saw us he started snaking through his ferret maze at warp speed.

"Welcome to Ferret World," Jason announced.

"No kidding!" I said.

Jason had set up half of the basement like an enormous ferret jungle gym. It looked like the coolest amusement park ever, but for ferrets . . . and Radley had the whole place to himself. There was a fluorescent-colored tube maze that Jason built all the way up to the ceiling. He'd taken fleece ferret hammocks and hung them in different layers so Radley could crawl up and jump down or bounce. There were even little tents on the ground with ferret balls rolling by.

For a teeny-tiny second, I wished I could be a ferret, just to try out Ferret World. "Radley probably doesn't ever get bored in a place like this," I told Jason.

"I think he's just putting on a show for you, Ave. Radley's usually way more mellow."

Then I got an idea. "Truth or dare?" I asked Jason.

"Hmm. Dare."

That was what I was hoping he'd say. "All right." I couldn't hide my smile. "I *dare* you to hold Radley up and pretend to be snowboarding with him?"

"WHAT?" Jason looked like he didn't know whether to laugh or be afraid . . . very afraid.

"Just do it," I insisted.

I helped him position Radley on top of a chair holding Radley's arms out like a boarder's. Jason posed like he was doing the same. "Now . . ." I grinned. "Say FLEAS!"

"Huh?" Jason looked up like a deer in the headlights and I snapped my camera.

"Hah! Gotcha!"

"Hey!" Jason protested.

"Sorry, I had to trick you." The truth of the matter was I really wanted to sneak a picture of Jason to e-mail home to the BSG but he'd been so uncooperative about pictures that trickery seemed the only way!

"Okay. My turn. Truth or dare?" Jason asked.

My stomach flipped. Uh-oh. I had NOT counted on this type of revenge. *Stupid, stupid, stupid!* I thought as my mind started racing over the possibilities of what Jason could ask me. "Truth!" I said quickly . . . even though I knew nothing was safe.

"Okay. How come on the gondola today you weren't mad at those guys?"

"What?"

Jason slinked Radley through his hands and avoided my eyes. "You know . . . when they were talking about you not looking like your dad . . . you just answered them. Even though they were kind of being jerks, don't you think?"

"Well, I dunno," I admitted. "I guess I never thought of it like that. I hear it all the time—I mean, I am adopted. So I don't look like my dad. Which is why those guys were confused."

"But it was pretty rude of them to say that." Jason seemed like he was trying very hard to explain a point that meant a lot to him as he gently put Radley back into his ferret gym.

I sighed. "Look, here's the thing. I know I could get mad that those kids weren't more . . ." I searched for the perfect word and then it came to me. "*Considerate.* But my mom always tells me that I am who I am. Sure, I'm adopted. And I'm also a Madden. I'm from Korea and I'd really like to go there someday to learn more about what it means to be Korean. I mean, you need to be proud of who you are . . . and, if *you're* proud of yourself, other people will be too. You know?"

Jason nodded. "That's so . . ."

"So . . . ?"

"Mature." He grinned.

Wow. I'd never ever in all twelve years of my life on this PLANET been called mature by someone *my age*! In fact, it was usually the opposite. I wanted to run up and hug him and then I thankfully came to my senses. No way. Way way WAY no way.

For about ten seconds neither of us said a word and the only sound in the room was Radley squirming around his gym. "Truth or dare?" I asked to break the strangeness.

"Um . . . truth."

Then finally I asked him the question that had been on my mind for days. "What happened to your parents?" I knew it was personal, but for some reason I also knew that Jason wouldn't mind talking about it to me. It was just one of those things . . . a gut feeling.

"I'm not sure, actually."

That wasn't the answer I was expecting. I opened my mouth to say *Sorry—never mind*, but then Jason started talking about it.

"I always thought my parents had these boring, boring jobs when I was little. My mom worked at the town library and my dad was a computer repair guy. We moved around a ton when I was younger, and Mom and Dad were always going away on 'business' and leaving me with my grandparents in Durango. I don't know what kind of business trips a computer dude and a librarian had to go on, but whatever. Then a bunch of years ago, when I was four, they said they were going camping and left me with my grandparents. The whole way there my mom seemed pretty upset though. She gave me an extra long hug good-bye, I remember. They left that day and drove into the woods, and then it was like . . . I dunno . . . they disappeared. I haven't heard from them since . . . and," he said quietly, "nobody has any clue about what happened to them. The police found their car with all their stuff in it but my parents were gone. No notes, no nothing."

The hair on the back of my neck was standing straight up. "What do you think happened?"

"Gramps thinks it might have to do with the government, but who knows, really. I keep wondering if they're alive . . . if they'll find me again someday. But I try not to get my hopes up. Besides, things have been pretty good for me here. I loved living with Gramps and Grammy, but they were getting too old to take care of a teenager. I still get to see them when I take the bus to Durango once a month. Anyway, the Hulberts are awesome. Grammy found them herself through social services and thought they'd be perfect for me. She was right. And Frankie's a great kid. I mean, it's hard to be new. But other than that, things are cool."

Jason's story would blow anyone else's I knew right out of the water. It was like something out of a movie. Now there was no doubt about it—Jason was seriously the bravest person I'd ever met. Who cared if he was shy around other kids sometimes? "I'm really glad you told me that, Jason."

"I've never told anyone before," he admitted.

"Well . . . your secret's safe with me," I promised. And it was.

"You want to go visit Ollie now?" Jason asked.

"Definitely!" Enough secrets and mushy stuff for one night—there was a red-tailed hawk to visit! I put on my coat and gloves but still felt kind of shivery. Something about being near this hawk gave me goose bumps. I couldn't imagine what Jason must feel like when he trained him.

As soon as we opened the door to the shed, I heard

Ollie fluttering on his perch. Jason pulled a string and the overhead light came on. It was dim, but we could see.

"There you are, Ollie." Jason spoke to Ollie like he was talking to a person. It was different from the funny way we talked to Radley and Marty. "Are you hungry?" Jason turned to me. "I was reading *Oliver Twist* when I found him. He was so hungry . . . he reminded me of Oliver." So that was how Ollie got his name! I wondered if Jason knew that an ollie was also a sweet boarding trick.

All of Jason's hard work feeding Ollie definitely seemed to be paying off. "I can't believe how big he is. I feel like he might be bigger than just a few days ago," I said.

"Yup. It's almost time to let him go. He needs to be free."

Jason put on his leather glove and started to pick up Ollie's swivel. I felt my heart beat faster. "Wait . . . are you freeing him tonight?"

Jason shook his head. "Nope. Tonight is just a little exercise. That's why I brought this." He held up an almost empty package of hamburger meat. "Ollie hasn't ever had to hunt for his own food in the wild, so as long as I keep a little burger with me he'll come right back."

Wow. Jason was so smart. His gramps sure taught him a lot about hawks.

We walked—quiet as mice—out of the shed with Ollie perched on Jason's left arm. Jason led us through the grove of trees to an open space, a frozen creek, and the River Trail. I didn't have any trouble seeing where I was going. The moon was almost full and—believe me—it was humongous! For some reason, the moon always looked bigger in Colorado. The whole way there, Ollie kept looking around like he was ready for his next adventure to begin. I knew just how he felt.

"Is it all right to let him fly at night?" I asked. Lucky me, I got to be in charge of holding the old package of hamburger. Gross!

"Usually we sneak out during the day. Sometimes I come home from school on my lunch break. But I haven't worked him today, and he needs the exercise."

Jason checked Ollie's anklets and jesses. Then he checked the swivel where they were attached, and he unclipped Ollie so he could fly free. I stood as still as a statue. The last thing I wanted was to startle Ollie as he started to practice.

Jason reached into his bag and took out a stick with a cord rolled around it, sort of like a ball of kite string. With one hand and his teeth he tied the string around what appeared to be a bunny stuffed animal with a bushy white tail. "This is the bait. Ollie goes right after it and brings it back to me."

"And gets a hamburger reward?"

"Exactly. He needs to be hungry when I fly him or he might keep going. The hunger will bring him back." Jason whirled the fake rabbit on a string around his head. It really was like a kite! It went higher and higher. When it was far enough away, Jason tossed Ollie off his fist. Ollie flapped his wings and flew upward after the lure.

Once he caught it, Jason let him take it farther, holding onto the stick and string. Then Jason blew a sharp blast on his whistle. He blew again. Ollie flapped down, feet first as he got closer. *Wham!* He landed on Jason's gloved fist—hard! I was surprised that Jason didn't fall over himself. But he only made a little flinching face when it happened. Otherwise he didn't even move!

"Atta boy. Good boy." Jason took a ball of the partly frozen hamburger, and tucked it into the *V* of his thumb and forefinger.

Immediately, Ollie bent down and pecked at the meat. His razor-sharp beak tore out chunk after chunk.

"It seems like he's almost ready to be released."

Jason nodded. "He is, and I have it all planned. I'm going to take him up Bear Creek for the release. It's near where I found him, so hopefully he'll fly right back to his friends and family."

I half smiled and looked at the lure. "Is Ollie going to think that rabbits fly?"

A smile crept onto Jason's face. "I hope not. But he'd go for a small bird, if it was slow enough. That's how hawks keep their prey healthy . . . by hunting for the weaker birds. It's the whole balance of nature thing."

"Just like wolves make deer or elk herds stronger by taking the sick or weak animals for food." I've read tons of books about wolves, and I even got to meet some face-to-face when I visited Montana with the BSG.

Jason smiled at me. "I've never met a girl who knows as much about animals as you do. It's . . . cool."

"I know!" I smiled back but then looked down. We were having so much fun, and it was like we barely even had to say anything. Was it possible to make a new best friend in just a couple of days?

Jason tossed the lure out one more time for Ollie, who

repeated his catch-the-flying-rabbit trick. As for me . . . well . . . I was beginning to wish this trip didn't have to end. I could've watched Jason fly Ollie all night, but it was getting colder and colder outside. Besides, Dad was coming at ten.

Jason and I headed back to the shed and put Ollie back where he belonged. I would've been way more nervous that Bonnie or Fred would find out, but Jason was as cool as a cucumber about keeping his hawk a secret.

As we walked back to the house, I thought about how to ask Jason the question that I'd been thinking about, well, pretty much all day. "Hey, the Snurfer is the day after tomorrow. . ." I began. "And I know you just started boarding, but . . . it would make me feel a lot better if—"

Jason suddenly looked crushed. "You don't want me to come? Would it make you nervous?"

Had Jason totally lost it? "No! Just the opposite! I want you to come. You're my only real friend here."

Jason grinned. "Phew. You didn't need to ask me, you know. I was going to come anyway. Your dad and I already talked about it today."

Dad! That explained his funny smile when we got back from the mountain.

I picked up the pace as I felt my cheeks get hot. Dad must have thought I had a crush on Jason—and I bet Tessa and Kazie did too! Well, they had it completely wrong. Jason and I were just friends . . . right?

Oh no, I thought, as an even more embarrassing idea slowly came together in my brain. I sneaked a glance over at Jason. Did he think I liked him . . . like *that*? And more importantly. . . did I?

18

Effective Edge

The next day I hit the slopes practically at sunrise—after a hearty breakfast, of course. As I raced down the Superpipe over and over again, willing myself to concentrate on my ollies and handplants, other thoughts somehow kept creeping in. Like while I was headed up the side of the pipe, all set to catch some air, my brain would be thinking "eggplant-eggplant-eggplant-Kazie-thinks-I-like-Jason-ahhhhh!" *Splat*. Total garage sale. It was soooo frustrating!

Finally, around three o'clock, I gave up on the practicing and headed back to the house. I'd gotten a few good runs in, and Dad always says too much practice the day before a big game—or competition—isn't good, anyway.

As I walked down the sidewalk carrying my board, I was totally missing the BSG. If I could have just spilled to Katani, or Maeve, or any of them, I knew I would feel one hundred percent better. My hand automatically went to my pocket, reaching for the little key ring Charlotte had given me. But the only thing there was a piece of candy. I checked the other pocket to be sure. My mouth felt dry. The pen and key ring were gone.

I tried not to panic and to think clearly. What if it had fallen out of my pocket on the pipe? In that case, it was totally and completely gone. But did I have it in my pocket before I headed out this morning? Think, think, think—where was the last place I remembered seeing the key ring? Then I remembered—the museum! I immediately changed course and headed for the big building with the green door, swallowing hard as I half ran/half speed-walked my way there. That was the last place I'd had the key ring—I was sure of it. My heart was aching! How had I managed to lose *two* of my special BSG gifts in only three days?

When I got to the museum I burst through the heavy door and stopped, panting. I must have looked pretty crazy, all out of breath and dragging a snowboard into a museum lobby.

"Is something wrong?" the woman behind the front desk asked, concerned.

"I lost my lucky key ring! My best friends in Boston gave it to me, and I have to have it in my pocket tomorrow for the Snurfer Competition. I was here last night, and I think maybe I left it here somewhere." The words spilled out. It was way more than the woman needed to know, but I wanted her to understand that this was urgent.

She smiled. "Let's look around. Do you think you lost it in the room where Cowboy Jack was speaking?"

"It has to be there. I know I had it then." I leaned my

board against the closest wall and leaped up the stairs, with the woman following.

She turned on lights, and I searched the storytelling room and the entire hall. No key ring. I felt like the whole world was caving in around me. The woman was very nice and promised to call if anything turned up, but how was that supposed to make me feel better? I was devastated. Totally, one hundred percent devastated. The Snurfer was tomorrow, after all.

As I dragged myself and my board back home I got more and more upset just thinking about everything. When I got home I ran into the house where Marty met me, bouncing and barking. "Oh, Marty. It's good to see *you*." I tried to grab him into a hug, but Marty would have none of that. He barked and wiggled free.

I felt like a balloon that had just been popped. Even Marty had deserted me!

Dad came out of the kitchen to see what Marty was making so much noise about. "Hey," he said, sounding concerned. "What are all these tears for?"

That's when I realized I was crying. Ugh. I never cried. Not really, anyway. Suddenly everything came spilling out.

"Okay, yesterday morning I couldn't find my Kgirl original ear warmer . . ."

"You mean that headband?"

"Headband, ear warmer, whatever. And then today, I realized my key ring from Charlotte is gone too! What else can go wrong? I'm probably going to make a total fool of myself in the Snurfer tomorrow. Dad, this *stinks*."

Dad gave me a big Dad hug. "Maybe this will cheer you up." He handed me a package. "I wrapped it myself."

"I can see that." The present was all bumpy and wadded up in a Snurfer poster. It made me laugh, even through my sniffles.

I slipped off the string and unrolled the poster. Inside was a light blue T-shirt. Best of all was the picture on the front. Dad had gotten the photo he took of me and him before we went boarding silk-screened on the front of the shirt. Beneath the picture, in big block letters, it read: THE SNURFS. This shirt said that Dad and I were best buds, as well as super snowboarders. I could hardly wait to wear it to school to show everyone how awesome my dad was.

I gave Dad a hug. "I love it! I'm going to put it on right now. If this doesn't help me win the Snurfer, I don't know what will!"

"Hey, but remember, Ave, it's not what you wear, it's how you—"

"Yeah, yeah, I know . . . it's how you snurf. Doesn't matter, Dad. This T-shirt is the coolest!" I was going to sleep in it for good luck.

Dad gave me another hug. "Try not to worry about the contest, Avery. Just do your best. You're going up against the top snowboarders in the state, you know."

I had a feeling he was talking about Kazie. Did that mean Dad thought I wasn't good enough? I felt a pinch in my stomach.

Dad went back to the kitchen to finish working on dinner. I snatched up Marty, ran upstairs, and flopped onto my bed. Maybe I would e-mail the BSG. I didn't have to mention the lost key ring or the ear warmer, right?

To: Katani, Maeve, Isabel, Charlotte
From: Avery
Subject: Snurfers Unite!

Hey guys! I've had the craaaziest
vacation ever! 2morrow is the Snurfer
and I gotta admit ... I'm kinda nervous.
Kazie (the gf's daughter) is wicked good.
Oh well. Wish me luck! Miss you!
Avery.
PS—Marty met an evil cat named Farkle—
more later.

CHAPTER

19

Method Air

O nce, when I was in fifth grade, we had to try out for
the A team and the B team for soccer. Soccer's always
been my super sports specialty. But that day in fifth
grade, I was so nervous I put on two pairs of socks. Seriously. I'm talking two socks on each foot. (Don't worry—I
still made the A team.) Now just to give you an idea, that
nervousness doesn't even come close to the butterflies in
my stomach on the morning of the Snurfer.

I ate a huge bowl of oatmeal with banana slices for
breakfast. I needed my power fuel more than ever. Then I
got dressed—with only one sock on each foot, I swear! As
I got into the car and buckled up, everything seemed okay.
So far, so good. I knew I was kind of fidgety, but I didn't
realize how much till Dad said, "Avery, tell me honestly.
Did you have Mexican jumping beans for breakfast this
morning?"

"I'm just excited!" I said. "Check out this pow-pow."

It was true. The snow all around us was thick and

sparkly. I was going to tear it up today on the pipe! I looked around for wood to knock on so I wouldn't jinx myself, but there wasn't any so I knocked on Dad's head.

He laughed and rubbed the spot where I knocked. "Well, if you're so excited already, then maybe I shouldn't tell you this . . ." he trailed off with a mysterious smile.

"What?" I replied immediately. "What is it? Come on, you can't just start to spill and then stop like that!"

Dad's grin got even bigger. "Well, if you must know . . . it just so happens that we have another 'surprise' celebrity judge. I wasn't sure if she was going to be able to make it, so I didn't want to announce it to everyone . . ."

When I heard "she," I got the chills. I knew exactly who it had to be. Only the most famous female snowboarder of all time. Only the 2006 silver medal winner in Snowboard Cross at the Olympics. Only—

"Lindsey Jacobellis!" I squealed. Dad laughed again as he pulled the car into the ski resort parking lot.

"Yep, that's the one," he informed me. "But don't let it make you nervous, okay, Ave? Just do your best."

Right, I thought. Just do my best in front of my IDOL.

When we got out of the car, Dad and I turned to each other and breathed at the same time, "Whoa." It looked like the set of a Hollywood movie. Ajax Mountain was always crowded, but now it was a total zoo. People swarmed all around—cameras and trucks were everywhere. I counted at least six TV stations.

As we unloaded the Snurfmobile, people kept coming up to Dad and shaking his hand. "Great job, Jake. This is going to be a truly momentous event," said a dude with a long curly beard wearing a TV station baseball cap.

"Jake Madden! The man, the myth, the legend!" shouted a lady in huge black sunglasses.

Dad just waved a little. I'd never seen him look so embarrassed! I tried to pass him his Snurfer hat, but he shook his head at me. Dad usually loved any chance to look silly in public. But today his brown hair was parted to the side and combed neatly, and instead of wearing his usual bright blue one-piece jumpsuit, he had on a new jacket that he must have picked up at ATS yesterday. The Snurfer was obviously a big deal to Dad—such a big deal that he was changing his whole "it's not about what you wear" rule! I really hoped I wasn't going to let him down.

"I have to go sit with the judges, Avery." Dad gave me a huge bear hug. "Good luck! And remember the most important thing . . ."

"Just have fun!" we shouted in unison.

Yeah, I thought, *that's easy for you to say!* I wanted to have fun, but that was before Crazie Kazie came into the picture. Everything was getting so confusing. Even though I didn't really want to, I was sort of starting to like her. But when it came to boarding, I still knew that we were definitely NOT on the same team.

I couldn't tell Dad, though. "I will," I promised. I hugged Dad and watched him walk away toward the judges' stand, where I thought I could make out two blond heads—the Golden Egg and Lindsey Jacobellis. The snowboarding star power at this event was way overwhelming! *Maeve would love all this celeb stuff*, I thought, suddenly missing that red-headed drama queen.

"Over here, Avery," said a voice behind me. There she was. Kazie looked even more bright and cheerful than usual, and that said something for the Telluride magenta queen! She'd upgraded her ribbon 'do to TWO ribbons per braid—pink and orange. She'd even put on glittery makeup so her cheeks shimmered like the snow. Normally I'd say that was way too girly for shredding, but for some reason Kazie could totally pull it off. She took my arm and steered me toward an official who was giving out numbers for the contestants to wear. "Can you believe the crowds? I'm super psyched. Aren't you?" she asked.

"Totally!" I answered. That was a big, whopping lie. Super nervous was more like it.

"I can't wait to get going," Kazie exclaimed.

"Me neither," I said. There went another lie. I was definitely having second thoughts.

"Good luck," Kazie told me with a pat on the back.

"Good luck to you too!" I told her. For once, that *wasn't* a lie. I totally meant it!

Kazie stuck out her hand, grabbed mine, and squeezed it. "You'll be great. I know you will. Your dad never stops talking about how great you are. I hope I can make him proud too."

I wanted to say something equally as nice, but before I had the chance, Kazie leaned her board up against a fence and hurried off to find her friends. The fence was covered with boards of every size and color, so I figured mine would probably be safest right next to its bright red ATS twin. I leaned my board beside Kazie's and smiled. If it weren't for our opposite bindings, those boards would've been practically identical. They looked awesome next to each other though . . . great advertising for the store.

"Hi, Avery."

I turned around. "Jason! Frankie! Wow, guys, thanks for coming!"

Jason smiled back, but Frankie didn't seem all that excited to be at the Snurfer. He held on tight to Jason's hand . . . which was definitely a good thing. If they got separated in this crowd, finding him again would be a nightmare!

"I brought you something for good luck," Jason said, reaching into his pocket. Luck! Could it be . . . did Jason have my ear warmer and my key ring after all? That would be too cool for words.

But instead, Jason handed me a piece of paper. The paper had a drawing of a ferret on a snowboard, doing a back flip. "It's Radley," he explained, as if I didn't already know.

"This is perfect. I definitely feel like good luck is on the way!" I folded the paper and tucked it into my pocket. Jason smiled. Real good luck wasn't in just one little object . . . it was just what made you feel lucky. The BSG would want me to feel happy because of their charms, not guilty because I misplaced them. I knew when I told them the story they would totally understand. And this picture from Jason meant tons of luck. "Thanks, Jason. This is exactly what I needed!"

A fuzzy noise began blaring from the loudspeakers.

"Hey, they're calling names. What number are you?" Jason looked at my armband. "Avery, you're number five! You gotta go!"

I grabbed my board and squeezed my helmet over my ears. "Okay, wish me luck!"

"Good lu—" he started, then looked frazzled. "Frankie? Oh, man, where's Frankie!? I gotta find him so we can get a good spot to watch you! Good luck, Avery. You'll do just fine." Jason waved and took off.

Watching from the stand with the other boarders, I could only see the first few moves of each contestant. It was weird being so early in the contest. Half of me wished I could hurry up and get it over with, but the other half wanted about five more people to go before me.

"Avery Madden." Finally, the speaker boomed my name, and something inside me took over. All around me the yelling and screaming and applause instantly faded away. Almost automatically, I waved to the crowd like I'd been doing this my whole life! I turned once to check out the judges' bench. There were about seven people sitting there, but I only noticed two—Dad and DK. They both waved at the same time and saluted—they probably planned it. Funny . . . veeeery funny. I took a deep breath and walked across the top of the pipe, laid my board on the snow, and stepped into the bindings.

No thinking allowed. Just fun. I imagined Marty flying on a board and this time he had company—a little brown Radley ferret. I was laughing again! I lifted my arms, leaned forward, and off I flew. As I picked up speed with my knees bent, I whooshed up the far side of the pipe.

The first time, I did a simple air-to-fakie. I approached the wall riding forward, and slid back down riding backward. Boom. Easy-peezy. Then I really started to pick up speed. I looked over my shoulder, caught big air, and did a backside handplant. I rotated 180 degrees and coasted forward down the pipe.

So far, so good. A simple alley-oop on the front side turned me to fly back down forward. The snow was so fresh that it made a crisp shredding sound as I carved. I guess that was how boarding got its nickname. I was feeling nice and warmed up now. I flipped back over into a frontside handplant, just as I'd done for Donnie when he was coaching me. Then I went for a ho-ho, grabbing my board with both hands. I finished my ride with a stellar, DK-approved eggplant. I slid to the bottom, did some butterflies, and threw one fist high into the air.

Suddenly the stands exploded into applause and whistles. A wave of relief passed over me. I'd made it. I let the cheering of the crowd sink in, and it was A-W-E-S-O-M-E! I felt like a superstar! At the judges' booth I saw Dad and DK. They were jumping up and down and hugging. "Yeah, Snurfette!" DK screamed. I laughed out loud. At that very moment in time I really didn't know how I'd done and I didn't even care. The most important thing was *I had fun.* After all, wasn't that what it was all about? I unclipped my board, tucked it under my arm, and waved one more time before heading back to the contestant stand where the boarders were hanging out.

I don't know how, but everyone who walked by me knew my name. "Great job, Avery." "You rocked it out there." "Sweet flying, Madden."

"Thank you, thank you. No autographs please, no

"The snow was so fresh that it made a crisp shredding sound as I carved."

autographs," I joked, but I didn't have time to stop and talk. I really wanted to see my friends. Now that the Snurfer was behind me I didn't have anything to worry about! I could just chillax with Jason, and even Kazie, and have fun for the rest of the trip.

When I got back to the top of the pipe, there was a giant huddle and everyone was shouting. All the voices sounded loud and angry, but there was one that was way louder than the others—Kazie's. I'd heard her at full blast enough to recognize her yell right away. "This is so UNFAIR!" she cried. "Why should I be punished because someone did something *horrible* to ME?"

Something horrible to her? I hoped everything was okay. I jogged up the hill as fast as I could. People saw me right away and the huddle broke in two parts. It was like what happened at the ice cream store to Kazie, only now I was the one walking through! Was it because I was a Snurfer celebrity? Uh-oh. From the angry looks on everyone's faces, I had a feeling it was bad. Very, very bad.

Tessa stepped out of the crowd and stomped toward me. I thought fire might shoot out of her eyeballs—that was honestly how mad she looked. "How could you?" she said.

How could I WHAT?

Kazie stood in the center of group. Her face was bright red, and her hair hung in tangles around her face. When she saw me, tears started to stream out of her eyes. It scared me a little. I'd never seen Kazie look anything other than brave and happy. "All right, where is it? Come on, Avery, I know it was you!"

My whole body was shaking. "What was me? What are you talking about?"

"You STOLE my ATS snowboard!" Kazie almost spat the words out.

"Yeah!" Siobhan popped out behind her. "It's so obvious it was you, Avery. You knew there was no way you could win if Kazie competed, so you took her board!"

Tessa shook her head and made her eyes real squinty. "And now Kazie's disqualified, *because of you*. It's supposed to be a *game*, Avery. A FUNDRAISER. Gosh, how immature can you be?"

The ground started to feel wobbly beneath me. "B-b—but, I didn't take your board, Kazie. I swear I didn't!"

"Why should I believe you?" Kazie said. Her voice was shaking.

"I'm not a cheater. I would never do that. Hey, you can use my board," I offered.

Now Kazie stopped crying altogether and folded her arms. Maybe my offer was a step in the wrong direction. "I *can't* do that. I'm goofy-footed, remember? You know what, just forget it! Leave me alone!"

I saw Dad, DK, and the rest of the judges march over from their booth to check out what all the fuss was about. I felt dizzy. There was no way I could take another person yelling at me over something I didn't do. I had to get out of there.

I slapped down my board, clipped one foot into it, and pushed off behind the halfpipe until I reached the ski run. I stepped into my other binding and flew over the moguls, zipping down the slope. The sound of music and cheering grew fainter the farther I boarded from the pipe.

I took the long way down the mountain and boarded until the tears on my face dried into ice crystals. No one was there at the bottom. The city was like a ghost town, silently waiting for the contest to be over and people to come down and celebrate.

I kicked out of my straps, grabbed my board, and ran all the way home. On the walk in front of Dad's house I slipped on the ice and fell down. My right knee hit the ground first, and even though it throbbed in the worst way, the idea that Kazie thought I'd done something so mean and horrible hurt way more. I left my board right there on the walk. I opened the front door and slammed it behind me with all my might. I knew I wasn't supposed to ever slam doors but no one was home and I plain old didn't care.

"I didn't do it!" I screamed out loud.

Marty trotted into the room, took one look at my face, and scampered over to give me kisses. He flew into my arms and licked my face.

"Talk about a mess," I whispered.

Just then I heard a *crunch crunch crunch* sound outside. Then a *DING DONG*. The doorbell. Who could be coming over now? I didn't want to see anyone! I slowly opened the door.

"Avery, can I talk to you?" Jason asked. I looked at the object he was clutching in his arms, and my heart ker-thumped. It was a *red ATS snowboard*. We stood there for what seemed like FOREVER.

Finally I burst. "Jason . . . *you* took Kazie's board?" Jason didn't say anything but his eyes got huge. "I hope you know, she thinks I did it!" I shook my head and felt my voice cracking. "Some friend you are . . ."

"Avery, wait—" he started.

"Well then, what?"

Jason opened his mouth but nothing came out. He shoved the snowboard at me and ran off, disappearing around the corner of the street.

20

Butterflies

I stood there for a minute holding the snowboard and shivering in the doorway. How had everything spun out of control so quickly? *I guess that's how it is with messes and fake friends,* I thought. One minute, everything's all neat and tidy, and the next—*SPLAT*—tomato sauce everywhere, or you're flat on your back on the mountain, or your snowboard's gone. But how could Jason do such a thing? I thought he was a friend . . . a best friend, even. Boy, was I wrong.

Just then I heard the sound of a motor and saw the Snurfmobile turning the corner onto Willow Street. Dad pulled into the driveway . . . and he wasn't alone. Andie was sitting in the passenger seat. Then, the van door slid open, and who should come tumbling out but Kazie. And, of course, in her arms was a squirming, twisting ball of fur. I'd never seen Kazie OR Farkle look so mad. I thought smoke might blow out of Kazie's ears at any second. And as for Farkle, well, from the way he was screeching . . . I was afraid that whatever evil demon lived inside of him was going to make an ugly appearance.

Kazie got to the door, glared, and pointed at my hand. "I KNEW IT!" she cried. That's when I realized I was still holding Kazie's board.

"Avery," Dad said. I could tell he was trying his hardest to keep his cool. "Your board is there on the walkway. Is that one Kazie's?"

My mouth was almost too dry to speak. "Yes."

Before I could explain, Kazie charged into the room with Andie right behind her. "My board!" Kazie tugged the snowboard from my arms. "How could you?" Tears streamed down her cheeks.

"Now, let's calm down," Dad instructed. "I'm sure there's a perfectly logical explanation for all of this," he added, but the look in his eyes said *I hope!*

"Avery, how come you have Kazie's snowboard?" Andie asked in a slow, shaky voice.

Kazie placed Farkle on the ground beside her and put her hands on her hips. The moment Farkle was loose, Marty ran to the den and scrambled to safety in an arm chair. Farkle, with his wacky eyes and messed-up ear, darted beneath the chair to wait it out. My heart was pounding, half for me and half for M-Dawg. "I didn't take it," I insisted. That was easy enough. The next part was the tricky one, but I took a deep breath and spat out the terrible truth. "Jason brought it over here. He just left before you guys came."

"Jason?" Kazie looked suspicious. "Why would *Jason* take my board?"

I shook my head. "I have no idea."

"But that doesn't make *any* sense!" Kazie exclaimed. "Jason barely even snowboards! He . . . he doesn't even *know* me!" She was talking faster and faster with her head moving back and forth. It was making me even more jumpy. "He has no reason to keep me out of the competition, unless . . ." Suddenly Kazie's face changed. "Unless he thought that if I didn't compete, *you'd* win."

I was about to argue and then it dawned on me—she could be right. That would be the only logical explanation for why Jason would take her board. I remembered what he'd said right before the Snurfer: *"You'll do just fine."* But never, in a million years, would I have thought Jason could do something so slimy to anybody. Even though he'd brought the snowboard back and practically confessed to the crime, I still didn't believe it . . . or didn't want to.

Kazie held a trembling finger up and pointed at me. "Was this your idea?"

I furiously shook my head. "Me? No! Are you kidding?"

She lowered her arm but glanced behind her for backup. Farkle knew his cue. He crept backward, leaned on his hind legs, and sprang forward. Just as he popped into the air, Marty leaped off the chair and pounced on Farkle's gnarly, striped tail. Farkle let out an ear-shattering "ROOOOOOOW, YEOOOOOOOW!"

I couldn't believe my eyes. Marty had totally nailed him! Farkle's paws scrabbled at the rug in fast-forward, but Farkle couldn't move an inch. Hah! The little dude was back and better than ever. I knew I could count on Marty. He always had my back.

Kazie, Andie, Dad, and I had to muffle down giggles. I took a deep breath and looked Kazie right in the eye. "Look. I never, ever told Jason to take your board. I just wouldn't do that, Kazie. Playing by the rules is . . . well . . . the only way *I* play." I saw Dad nod approvingly. It was good to know he believed in me, but I knew that if I wanted Kazie to really trust me, I had to tell her the full story. Even if it was kind of embarrassing. Sometimes you just need to get over it. "Kazie, I admit, maybe I was a little . . ." I stopped for a second, hating that I had to say this next word. ". . . *jealous* of you. You're a really, really awesome snowboarder. But I knew I couldn't win the competition. I just wanted to have fun and do my best. Whatever Jason thought, that was his idea. I never put him up to it. I swear."

Kazie was quiet for a second, then finally said, "I believe you." She walked into the den and collapsed onto the couch looking totally zonked. I knew just how she felt.

"Kazie," Andie suggested softly. "I think you owe Avery an apology."

Kazie sighed. "I'm sorry. I shouldn't have yelled at you like that. I was just so mad that I didn't get to compete . . . especially because someone stole my board. It was so completely unfair."

"It was," I agreed. "I wish all of it had never happened."

Kazie nodded. "Me too. And to tell you the truth, I was kind of jealous of you, too. I mean, you came here out of nowhere and all of a sudden all anyone would talk about was the Snurfman's funny, cool daughter. I guess part of me wanted them all to think that you weren't as great as they thought. I'm really sorry." Marty scurried over to Kazie and licked her face, making her smile a little. After his Farkelator victory, he wasn't afraid to go near Kazie anymore.

"I'm not mad," I told her. "I just feel bad that you didn't get to compete in the Snurfer."

Kazie shrugged. "Aw, Snurfer Shmurfer. I mean, it wasn't sanctioned, so I didn't lose any points. There'll be other competitions. Besides, it was just for fun." She sniffled away her last tears and gave me a smile.

"Avery, I have some good news for you, though," said Dad, laying a hand on my shoulder. "You placed. You came in fifth!"

I whipped around. "Are you kidding me? I got fifth!" I started jumped up and down and throwing punches in the air before I thought to calm down a little. (You know— to be a little more thoughtful of Kazie.) They were all laughing, though. I think we knew that if Kazie had gotten to compete she'd be doing a first-place dance herself.

"DK wanted me to tell you to write more postcards to your friends about your Snurfer glory," Dad said. Huh, those postcards . . . whatever happened to them?

"I even got pictures!" Dad added and handed me the digital camera. Talk about some sweet shots! I was airborne in most of them. There was my frontside handplant. I clicked to the next picture, and there I was executing a flawless alley-oop. Then I clicked ahead again and felt a pang of sadness. It was the one I tried to take of Jason at Legends and Lore, when he moved Frankie in front of the camera. Frankie was sitting on Jason's shoulder and almost completely blocking his face, but I zoomed in to see if Jason was smiling. Then I noticed something weird. I zoomed in some more. No way. It couldn't be . . . or could it?

Dad patted me on the back. "I think we all need some hot chocolate. And some dinner."

"Wait!" I cried. "Dad, look at this!" I handed him the camera. Coming out of Frankie's jacket pocket was a very familiar-looking piece of blue fabric. MY KGIRL ORIGINAL EAR WARMER. How did it get there? And more importantly . . . why?

"Is that what I think it is?" Dad asked. Andie and Kazie stared at us, curious about what was going on.

"My ear warmer! I mean headband! Well, whatever it is, it's *right there* in Frankie's pocket." I was getting really wound up now. "Which means maybe Jason wasn't the one who took the snowboard after all!"

Kazie's eyes lit up. "You mean Frankie could have taken it, just like he took your stuff?"

"Exactly."

Dad glanced at Andie. "Look, we need to get to the bottom of this, and the sooner the better. There've been a lot of accusations made this afternoon, without a whole lot of facts to back them up. It's always important to find out the truth before you start pointing fingers at anyone." Now Dad was looking at both Kazie and me.

"Let's take a ride over to the Hulberts', Avery," he suggested. "I think you need to talk to Jason and find out his side of the story."

"Right now?" The words slipped out of my mouth. I

was embarrassed about how I'd exploded at him when he brought back the snowboard. I guess Kazie and I had more in common than just boarding after all.

"Now is the best time—while everything's fresh."

I knew he was right. I owed Jason a big-time apology. And Frankie, as Ricky Ricardo says on *I Love Lucy*, had some 'splainin' to do! Dad and I put on our coats and told Andie and Kazie that we'd be back soon. They understood. No need for everyone to come along.

It was a short ride to Jason's house. The sun was going down and now the streets were filled with people celebrating. It seemed like everyone outside of the Snurfmobile was yelling and cheering, but inside we were quiet. It had been a long and confusing day.

When we got to the Hulberts', Dad rapped firmly on the door. Bonnie opened it, wearing an apron smudged with yellowy goop. "Jake! Avery! What a nice surprise!"

"Bonnie, we have a little . . . " Dad's voice got quiet. ". . . *situation* on our hands." We kicked off our shoes and stood in the hall.

Bonnie smiled politely and led us into the dining room. "I just made a banana coconut cake . . . would you like a piece?"

"Absolutely," said Dad. I shot him a look. He shrugged. "What?"

How could Dad think about cake at a time like this? But I wasn't exactly disappointed when Bonnie cut me a piece of creamy, cakey deliciousness. Fred and Frankie were sitting at the kitchen table, but Jason was nowhere in sight.

"So, what's up?" asked Bonnie.

Dad coughed and looked at Frankie.

Fred understood. "Frankie," he said, "why don't you run up and put on your pajamas? I'll be up in a minute to tuck you in."

Frankie hesitated but obeyed. I remembered how Jason said Frankie was like a wounded animal, and right now he reminded me of one more than ever—all shaky with his head down.

Once he was gone, Dad took out the camera and showed Bonnie and Fred the picture with my ear warmer. He explained what happened with Kazie's snowboard that day and the possible misunderstanding when Jason came to drop it off. "We think maybe Frankie might have something to do with it," Dad said gently.

I waited for this news to sink in, figuring that when it did, Bonnie and Fred would start yelling for Frankie to "get down here at once!" Instead, they sat at the table quietly and glanced at each other. Finally Bonnie spoke. "Frankie's had trouble adjusting to family life, Avery. He bonded to Jason immediately—Jason's so good with him. But when you started coming around the house, Frankie began acting out. I think he's jealous of your friendship with Jason."

Fred sighed. "I wish I could say I was surprised, but Frankie's taken little things from school before, and once or twice from other kids' houses. The school psychologist says it makes him feel a sense of belonging. We know it's a problem. But I still don't know why he would take Kazie's board—he hardly knows her."

Suddenly we heard a creaking sound from the stairs and the kitchen door swung open. Frankie stood there wearing red footie pajamas, holding my ear warmer and key ring. He stared at the floor.

"Here," he said quietly, holding out my stuff without looking up at anyone. He slid a fleece-covered foot back and forth across the floor. How could it be possible for a little thief to be so cute? Seeing him like that, with his hair all messy and that guilty look on his face, made my heart melt. I knew what he'd done was wrong, but I couldn't be too mad. I walked over and kneeled down in front of him, taking the items from his little hands.

"It was wrong to take these, Frankie," I told him.

"I know," he whispered.

I felt really bad for the little guy, but I had to ask. "Did you . . . take anything else?"

"Um . . . yeah," he said finally, still looking down at the floor.

"Did you take Kazie's snowboard?"

He looked up at me quickly. "No, I took *your* snowboard!" So that was it—he thought he was hiding *my* board! I almost burst out laughing, but then I thought of Kazie. She probably wouldn't think his mistake was very funny. I held in my laughter and tried to put on my most serious face.

"No, Frankie," I told him firmly, "that was Kazie's. Our snowboards look exactly the same—except they have special settings so that Kazie can only ride hers, and I can only ride mine. When you took Kazie's board, you took away her chance to win the Snurfer. And, you hurt my feelings—and Jason's."

Frankie's eyes widened as I explained what he had done. "I'm really sorry!" he said very sincerely, looking like he might burst into tears at any moment.

"You have to promise never to do this again," Fred said in a stern but understanding voice as he bent down to scoop Frankie into his arms.

Frankie nodded solemnly. It really seemed like he had learned his lesson.

"Well, in that case . . ." I handed Frankie the key ring with the charms and froggie pen. "Why don't you keep this . . . for good luck. I have plenty of pens back home." I knew the BSG would want me to do that.

Frankie began to smile. "Wow, really? Coooool!" Dad smiled and rubbed my shoulder. I decided to keep the ear warmer . . . it was more like a headband, really. "Thanks, Avery!" Frankie said. I think he was happier that I wasn't mad than he was about getting a present.

"Now, do you know where Jason is?" I asked Frankie. "I guess I need to say I'm sorry to him."

Frankie shrugged. "Jason's gone."

Bonnie and Fred glanced nervously at each other and Bonnie said very slowly, "What do you mean?"

Frankie looked up. "He left. Time to say good-bye to Ollie." In an instant, Frankie realized what he'd said, and slapped his hand over his mouth. "Uh-oh . . ."

Uh-oh was right. "Where's Jason? Who's Ollie? Will somebody please fill me in?" Bonnie asked. Her eyes were full of panic.

Fred put Frankie down and dashed up the stairs. A moment later he pounded back down. "He's not in his room. I'll call the police station. They'll get the patrol car out there ASAP."

Then it hit me. "Wait! I know where he is, Bonnie. I'm sure I do." I pushed my chair back and jumped up.

"Where?" Bonnie sounded like she was on the verge of tears.

"Bear Creek," I answered honestly. I didn't want to be the one to tell her everything about Ollie—Jason's big secret—and maybe, just maybe, I wouldn't have to. "Jason's taking care of an injured hawk . . . from Bear Creek."

"Jason and his creatures." Bonnie's voice was squeaky. "But Fred, you can only get to Bear Creek by those old logging routes, and you can't drive the patrol car on the logging routes in this season."

"I have an idea," I said, but no one was listening.

"There's a big snowstorm coming tonight," Fred noted.

Bonnie clasped her hands together. "What are we going to do?"

"I HAVE AN IDEA!" I didn't know I was shouting until I noticed that all eyes had suddenly turned to me. "Snowmobiles can get through those logging routes, no sweat. Dad has a snowmobile in the back of the van. Dad and I can go out there and get Jason. It'll be a piece of cake." I looked at Dad. "Please?"

"Are you sure that's really where Jason is, Avery?" Bonnie asked.

"Yes." I nodded. "I'm almost a hundred percent sure."

Fred looked at Bonnie. "If that's what Avery thinks, it's our best bet."

Dad sighed. "All right. We'll go. Fred, you and Bonnie stay here in case he comes back."

We put on our coats and told Fred and Bonnie not to worry. "If I know Jason . . . he'll be there," I promised.

The snowflakes hit as soon as we started driving. They were big and wet, perfect snowball flakes. The sun had disappeared behind the mountains. I knew in another half hour it would be totally dark except for the light of the moon. "Who's Ollie?" Dad asked as he drove further out of the town center.

I knew I could tell Dad what was up. He deserved to know the truth. Plus, after tonight, Ollie would be back in nature where he belonged. "Ollie's a hawk . . ." I began. As we drove to Bear Creek, I explained the story of Ollie, right down to how he got his name.

We parked the car next to the River Trail at the south end of town. The snowmobile was heavy. Even though Dad was strong, he still needed my help lifting it from the van.

Dad took his place in the driver's seat and I took mine behind him. "Ready?" Dad asked.

I put on my helmet and wrapped my arms tightly around his waist. "Ready." I leaned my head against Dad's back and held on tight.

Dad turned the key, and the motor cut the stillness of the woods with a loud *VROOM VROOOOM!* The snowmobile blasted like a cannon, sending a fountain of snow into the air behind us. We drove about half a mile into the woods, when I saw the reflection of the large yellow moon on the frozen river and Jason on a rock. "Dad, I'm afraid the snowmobile might scare Ollie. Can we stop, and I'll walk the rest of the way? You'll still be able to see me."

Dad parked the snowmobile and the motor made a dull purr. "I don't know, Ave. Are you sure I should stay here? Jason's okay?"

"I know he is, Dad. You just have to trust me." I put my hands on my hips.

Dad shut off the engine. The only sounds around us were the Rocky Mountain wind rattling the tree branches and the hooting of owls. "You have your watch on?" Dad asked. "I'll give you fifteen minutes. Make sure you stay on the path where I can see you."

"Deal." I gave him a quick hug and tramped off through the snow. It was only a few inches deep with sticks and old leaves underneath, so it wasn't too slippery. The full moon made the white path gleam.

It didn't take long for me to reach Jason sitting on the huge rock. Ollie was perched on his gloved fist wearing a little leather hood. Ollie heard me first. He flapped in my direction and let out a squawk. Jason turned. When he saw me he stared down at the ground.

I walked toward him and gulped. "Jason, I'm really sorry. I should've listened to you. I know Frankie took Kazie's board."

He slowly looked up. His blue eyes were brighter than

ever. In the moonlight, they looked almost glow-in-the-dark. "I'm so, so sorry," I repeated.

Jason shook his head. "Don't be."

Ollie fluttered on Jason's arm. "Seems like he's ready to go," I said gently. I knew that letting go of Ollie was going to be really tough for Jason. And would he even want me to be here, now that I had basically slammed the door in his face?

Jason sighed. He untied Ollie's hood and lifted it off. Then he untied the jesses and leash. I heard him swallow with every step of the process. I couldn't imagine letting go of a pet I loved. But then again, Ollie wasn't really a pet. He was meant to be free. Jason slipped off Ollie's anklets and lifted the hawk into the air.

"Okay, Ollie." Jason's voice was faint. He stretched his arm high above his head. "Go on, Ollie. Good luck."

For a second, Ollie hesitated. Then, flapping his enormous wings, he lifted off with almost no sound at all. Ollie lowered his wings slowly, raised them, and repeated, lifting himself up, up, up.

Jason looked happy and sad at the same time as he watched Ollie soar. I thought I saw a single tear slip out of the corner of his eye and drip down his cheek, but it could've been anything—a snowflake, a trick of the moonlight, even my imagination. I felt pretty uncomfortable—did he want me to go away and let him do this alone?

Suddenly, without taking his eyes off the sky, Jason reached over and grabbed my hand.

"I'm glad you're here," he whispered.

My heart was beating a million miles a minute, and I

"Above us, Ollie made two magnificent circles. *It's like he's saying good-bye,* I thought."

could feel my cheeks burning. I didn't know what to do or say. *I was holding hands with a boy!*

After a couple of seconds I blurted the first thing I could think of—"Me too." But it was totally true. This was one of those once-in-a-lifetime moments that I was sure I'd remember forever.

Our faces were tilted to the sky, and we blinked the snow out of our eyelashes. Above us, Ollie made two magnificent circles. *It's like he's saying good-bye,* I thought.

Then he was gone. We stood there without saying a word, and I felt the warmth of Jason's hand in the stillness of the cold night. Although the moment was kind of sad, I couldn't help smiling—just a little.

Finally, Jason turned back to the path. "We should go. Your dad will be worried." He held my hand for a full two minutes as we walked back through the snowy path. When Dad waved, he gave it one quick squeeze and then it was back to the pockets. But that was okay by me. I'd had enough explaining to do for one day. What happened on Bear Creek would be between Jason and me.

"Just in time." Dad tapped his watch. "Everything okay?"

"Yup. Everything's fine," I said and scooted onto the back of the snowmobile. Jason hopped on behind me.

"Great," Dad said, then twisted halfway around to face us. "Just one thing, Jason—no more taking in wild creatures, okay? Wild things need to be wild, and there are plenty of professionals around here who can help them if they need it." Dad's voice was firm but warm. I knew he understood how Jason felt about Ollie—like by helping him get better, maybe Jason had healed a little bit too.

"Sure thing, Mr. Madden," Jason agreed. I didn't think he'd want to keep such a mega-huge secret again anytime soon, anyway.

Dad gave us a wink and the snowmobile roared to life. He was so cool that way—I knew he wouldn't say another word about Ollie, or anything else.

As we drove off into the forest, the snowflakes stuck to my cheeks and the air was getting colder, but I felt toasty and warm. The full moon, round and perfect, glowed like a lightbulb in the black sky. It had been a craaaazy trip to Telluride, with Dad and Andie, Kazie, Farkle, the Snurfer . . . but it was definitely a week I wouldn't forget. I was proud that I'd made the trip all by myself, and I was reminded of Ollie, who was finally ready to fly off alone by himself, too. Then I thought of Frankie safe at home with Fred and Bonnie, and finally me, snug between Jason and Dad. All of us had something in common—we were right where we needed to be.

Epilogue

Flinging my bags on the floor, I flew across my bedroom. Kneeling down at Frogster's terrarium and Walter's cage so we were face-to-face, I could see in Walter's shiny reptilian eyes that he was as happy to see me again as I was to see him. Snakes have feelings too!

Ping! An e-mail already? I had just walked in the door!

```
To: Avery
From: BSG
Subject: Postcards


Dear Avery,
We're in the Tower Room right now and we
have a question. All of us got postcards
from Telluride that are signed by DK . . .
Char says that's a famous snowboarder. Is
that for real? How are things with Kazie?
```

Did she end up being cool? We can't wait
for you to come home. Maeve wants to know
if you're meeting any cute boys . . .
should we throw a pillow at her for you?
Miss you tooooons!!!

xoxox,
Isabel, Charlotte, Katani, and Maeve
PS—Who's Snurfette?

I immediately started typing to fill them in on all the
craaaaazy details of my trip—then I stopped, deleted
everything I'd written so far, and started over. There was
really only one way to share a story like this.

To: BSG
From: Avery
RE: Postcards

Dudes:
Friday night. Tower sleepover. You'll get
the whole Snurf-tastic 411, I promise!

Shred on,
Snurfette

To be continued . . .

"Sweet air, Shred Betty!"

Freestyle with Avery

BOOK EXTRAS

Freestyle with Avery ᵗᴿⁱᵛⁱalicious triVia

1. What's the name of the snowboarding competition that Avery has been dreaming about for months?
   A. The Pow-Pow
   B. The Snurfer
   C. The Telluride Challenge
   D. The Boarder Boogie

2. What charms are on the key ring Charlotte gives Avery?
   A. Basketball, dog bone, duckie pen
   B. Snowman, Eiffel Tower, doggy pen
   C. Snowboard, soccer ball, froggie pen
   D. Cowboy hat, half moon, kitty pen

3. According to Avery, who makes the best burgers in Telluride?
   A. Andie
   B. Scott
   C. Her dad
   D. Robbie

4. What is Donnie Keeler's snurf-tastic nickname?
   A. The Silver Streak
   B. The Platinum Board
   C. The Golden Egg
   D. The Bronze Bacon

5. What kind of bird is Ollie?
   A. A spotted owl
   B. A red-tailed hawk
   C. A bald eagle
   D. A crested hawk

6. Who teaches Jason the basics of snowboarding?
   A. Avery
   B. Donnie Keeler
   C. Crazie Kazie
   D. Avery's dad

7. What funny image does Avery focus on to help her do an eggplant for the first time?
   A. Farkle on a pair of skis
   B. Her dad wearing his jester's hat
   C. Marty on a snowboard
   D. Donnie Keeler eating a waffle mountain

8. What nail-biting tale does Cowboy Jack tell at Legends and Lore?
   A. The Story of Cindy Sedona
   B. The Legend of Candy McDougal
   C. The Tale of Sandy MacPhee
   D. The Saga of Annie Canary

9. What is Donnie Keeler's dog named?
   A. Bud
   B. Thud
   C. Mud
   D. Crud

10. What is Andie particularly bad at?
    A. Cooking
    B. Swimming
    C. Skiing
    D. Tying her shoes

Avery Madden

Avery's Snurfworthy Shredding Glossary

Air-to-Fakie: (p. 42)–A trick in which the boarder takes off from the top of a snow wall, riding forward, and lands riding backward without turning around in the air.

Alley-Oop: (p. 42)–Any maneuver in the halfpipe in which the boarder rotates 180 degrees or more in an uphill direction.

Backside: (p. 125)–Riding turned to face up the hill; done on the toes.

Blindsided: (p. 116)–When the boarder's movements and visibility are limited or restrained.

Blue Square: (p. 36)–A medium-difficulty slope to ski or board on.

Bonking: (p. 40)–Hitting an object (like another snowboard) with your snowboard.

Bunny Slope: (p. 108)–The super-easy hill where beginners can learn and practice.

Butterflies: (p. 126)–A trick in which the boarder lifts up the front of her board while riding and goes in a circle.

Chicken Salad Air: (p. 6)–A trick in which the boarder's rear hand reaches between the legs and grabs the heel edge between the bindings, keeping the front leg straight.

Crippler: (p. 40)–A sweet trick in which the boarder rides forward up the halfpipe wall, becomes airborne, rotates 90 degrees, flips over, rotates another 90 degrees, and lands riding forward.

Crud: (p. 98)–Varied, inconsistent, slushy, or icy snow; snow that's not sweet to ride.

Dice: (p. 121)–What you say when someone smoothly nails a complicated trick.

Digger: (p. 65)–When a boarder takes a really bad wipeout and is injured. It's called "digger" because of the body digging into the ground.

Double Black Diamond: (p. 38)–One of the most difficult and dangerous slopes to ski or board on, appropriate only for really advanced skiers or boarders.

Effective Edge: (p. 173)–The length of metal edge on the snowboard that touches the snow.

Eggplant: (p. 124)–A one-handed, 180-degree invert, in which you turn in the air and put your front hand on the lip of the halfpipe wall.

Fakie: (p. 42)–A term for riding backward.

Faceplant: (p. 123)–To fall with your face flat in the snow.

Frontside: (p. 126)–Riding turned to face down the hill; a frontside turn is done on your heels.

Garage Sale: (p. 123)–Messing up a trick on the pipe and falling on your face.

Glading: (p. 61)–Riding through the trees.

Gnarly: (p. 123)–Sweet. Just plain-old sweet.

Goofy-Footed: (p. 54)–Riding on a snowboard with the right foot in the forward position.

Grab: (p. 44)–Grabbing your snowboard with one or both hands.

Green Circle: (p. 109)–An easy slope to ski or board on; good for grommets.

Grommet: (p. 34)–A small, young snowboarder.

Halfpipe: (p. 42)–A snow structure built for freestyle snowboarding in which boarders can catch air and perform tricks by riding back and forth from wall to wall.

Hammer: (p. 120)–To ride as hard as possible.

Handplant: (p. 126)–A halfpipe trick in which the rider does a handstand on one or both hands.

Hardcore: (p. 121)–Sweet, awesome, challenging; especially when referring to a trick.

Ho-Ho: (p. 50)–A two-handed hand plant.

Hucker: (p. 120)–A boarder who throws herself wildly through the air and does not land on her feet.

Indy: (p. 126)–A grab of the toe edge with the back hand.

Knee Rocket: (p. 116)–A little kid who skis and doesn't know how to stop.

Backside air: (p. 120)–For this trick the boarder goes off a jump and twists 540 degrees (one and a half circles) in the air.

McTwist: (p. 120)–A trick in which the athlete approaches the halfpipe wall riding forward, goes airborne, rotates a backside 540 air, and lands riding forward. This trick was named after its inventor, skateboarder Mike McGill.

Melon: (p. 126)–A grab of the heel edge with the front hand with both legs bent evenly.

Method: (p. 126)–A grab of the heel edge with the front hand, bending both knees and pulling the board to head level.

Mute: (p. 126)–A grab of the toe edge with the front hand.

Nose: (p. 42)–The front tip of the snowboard.

Ollie: (p. 33)–A trick used to get air without jumping by lifting the front foot, then raising the rear foot and springing off the snowboard tail.

Pop Tart: (p. 121)–Airing from fakie to forward in the pipe with no rotation.

Roast Beef: (p. 126)–A trick in which the rider reaches between the legs, grabs the heel edge between the bindings, and holds the rear leg rigidly straight.

Rodeo Flip: (p. 151)–An invert done riding fakie or forward in which the rider rotates frontside or backside while flipping.

Rolling down the windows: (p. 122)–A boarder's attempt to stop herself from losing her balance in the pipe by waving her arms wildly.

Shred Betty: (p. 55)–An awesome female boarder.

Stalefish: (p. 126)–A grab of the heel edge with the back hand.

Sick: (p. 40)–Anything awesome in the snowboarding universe.

Slob Air: (p. 42)–Grabbing the nose of the snowboard.

Snurfer: (p. 3)–The first snowboard invented by Sherman Poppen in 1965. Poppen got the idea on Christmas day when his daughter wanted to sled standing up. He ran inside, bound two skis together, and tied a string to the nose so the rider could have control. Poppen's wife thought of the name "Snurfer" as a combination of "snow" and "surf." Soon everyone in the neighborhood wanted a Snurfer, and in the 1970s Poppen held the first Snurfer Competition.

Tail: (p. 114)–Rear of the snowboard.

Tuck: (p. 37)–A position in which the boarder crouches with her knees bent to achieve less wind resistance.

Wet Cat: (p. 121)–A midair flip with one hand on the lip of the pipe, rotating forward 90 degrees and landing riding backwards.

Glossary courtesy of Telluride Ski Resort.

www.TellurideSkiResort.com

Good Golly, It's Ollie!

An Avery Madden Crazy Critters Exclusive

When you hear the word "raptor," do you think of a small, toothy dinosaur? Well, *those* raptors have been extinct for about, oh, eighty million years or so, but plenty of raptors are still making a squawk today! Yup, many of today's predatory birds are called raptors too. Today we'll be talking to a very special member of this meat-loving bunch: my friend Ollie the red-tailed hawk.

Avery Madden: **So, Ollie. Do you feel at all nervous about your upcoming release into the wild?**

Ollie Hawk: Puh-lease! We hawks were *born to be wild*. Even if we've gotten used to falconry, we can revert to a semiwild state with only a little help from our human friends.

AM: **Wait a minute. I thought you were a red-tailed hawk! What exactly is this falcon stuff?**

OH: Well, falcons and hawks are both raptors, but it's true—we're not the same. And falconry isn't just about falcons. It's actually the practice of training any bird of prey to hunt or pursue game.

AM: **Cooool. So birds can be trained to hunt food for people? That's generous of you guys.**

OH: Whoa, there's been a misunderstanding. I expect to be paid for my services. I may be a bird, but I'm still an entrepreneur. The falconer trades me a piece of ready-to-eat meat for the fresh game I catch. I have a serious weakness for fast food.

AM: **Whatever floats your feathers, Ollie. Hey, speaking of feathers, I noticed your tail doesn't have the famous red-tailed hawk rusty red color. What's up with that?**

OH: Simple. Adults' tails are rusty red, and I'm not fully grown yet. Look into my eyes if you don't believe me.

AM: **That's okay . . . I believe you.**

OH: No, seriously. See the yellow in the irises of my eyes? That means I'm not completely mature yet.

AM: **So I take it there's no special someone in your life right now?**

OH: We hawks usually wait to date until after we shed our baby feathers–you know, to make sure we're looking our snazziest.

AM: **And when you do settle down . . . ?**

OH: I just want the same as any other red-blooded American: a tree in a nice neighborhood, three eggs, and a cozy nest.

AM: **Flap happy, Ollie!**

Avery's Avalanche of Craaazy Colorado Factoids

"This is a stick-up!"
The famous western bandit Butch Cassidy committed his first bank robbery in Telluride, Colorado, in 1889, getting away with more than twenty thousand dollars!

It's a red state?
In Spanish, Colorado means "reddish-colored," a name originally given to the reddish-looking Colorado River that runs through the state. When the state's Capitol building was constructed in the 1890s and early 1900s, builders used a rare marble called Beulah Red to honor their namesake color. But they might have gone a teensy bit overboard, using up all the Beulah Red Marble in the world during construction! Bet they were pretty *red-faced* after that.

The City of Lights
Think you know where the "City of Lights" is located? Think again! Although Paris, France, is often called the "City of Lights" today, Telluride, Colorado, was given the distinctive title back in 1892 when it became the first city ever to have electric street lights. *Ooh la la!*

How spooky is this?

Mining booms in the late 1800s brought tons of people to Colorado towns (like Telluride) to harvest the natural resources, including silver, uranium, radium, and gold. But when people discovered richer sources in other parts of the world, most of those settlers skedaddled just as quickly as they arrived, leaving almost as many ghost towns in the state (about 500) as live ones (650)!

You go, girls!

Colorado may be famous for its cowboys, but it's also seen some pretty exceptional cow*girls*. Katharine Lee Bates wrote the lyrics to "America the Beautiful" after being inspired by the view from Pikes Peak in Colorado.

He loves me, he loves me not . . .

Hundreds of thousands of valentines are mailed each year from Loveland, Colorado, through the town's Valentine Remailing Program. People from all over the country send in pre-addressed valentines, and local volunteers spend hours carefully marking each valentine with a special Loveland stamp. You can be sure that when these Loveland-labeled love letters reach their recipients, they're a real special delivery!

Share the Next

BEACON STREET GIRLS

Special Adventure

Katani's Jamaican Holiday

A lost necklace and a plot to sabotage her family's business threaten to turn Katani's dream beach vacation in Jamaica into stormy weather!

CHAPTER

1

An Important Letter

My dear Ruby,

I know it has been a long time since I have written. I do hope you and the family are well. In your letters to me over the years you have always expressed a desire to visit Jamaica, the home of your mother's birth, and I would so love to see you before the days run out.

My bakery is doing well. Though it is small, it keeps body and soul together. I bake a very tasty banana bread—nice and moist and flavorful. Truth is I can't produce enough to fill the demand. Everybody loves Nana's Banana Bliss.

Well, for some time I have been putting off some surgery, but can't do so any longer. On the 15th I will be going into the hospital. Now don't worry. It's just something I need to take care of. But I will have to close the bakery because the young girl who's there just can't manage on her own. The rest of the family can't really help out. I couldn't bring in a stranger.

But I really don't want to close it and lose my cus-
tomers or my growing momentum.

Another bakery has been trying to cut me out
of the business. You see, there's a man, Mr. Biggs,
who owns this bakery, and he has offered to buy me
out. He only wants to use my famous name, Nana's
Banana Bliss, to sell his cheaper, not better, banana
bread. I've made it known that I am not selling to
that man, so he has been trying every which way
to steal my customers and force me out of business.
What do you think of someone who would do such a
thing to an old woman like me? If I close the bakery,
even for a week, I'm afraid it will give him just the
opportunity he needs to destroy our business.

I know you are a busy person. We are so proud
of you, Principal Ruby, but my dear, we need your
help desperately. Do you think you could get some
time off, even just a week, while I have surgery, to
come and supervise the bakery for me? I would be
really very grateful, and as I said, it would be very
nice to finally meet you. And if you like, please bring
one of your granddaughters along. Jamaica is such
a beautiful place to visit, and it is the home of your
ancestors.

> *I am,*
> *Your loving aunt*
> *Faith*

Grandma Ruby finished reading, took off her glasses, and
set them down on our kitchen table with a little sigh. When
she looked up at me she had a faraway look in her eyes. I
glanced at the letter with the Jamaican stamp she was holding

and wondered if anything was wrong. But before I could say anything, Grandma cocked her head to one side and asked, "Katani, how would you like to go with me to Jamaica?"

Hello! Visions of beautiful beaches, palm trees, and pineapple drinks with little umbrellas began swirling through my brain.

Collect all the BSG books today!

#1 Worst Enemies/Best Friends   ☐ **READ IT!**
Yikes! As if being the new girl isn't bad enough . . . Charlotte just made the
biggest cafeteria blunder in the history of Abigail Adams Junior High.

#2 Bad News/Good News   ☐ **READ IT!**
Charlotte can't believe it. Her father wants to move away again, and the
timing couldn't be worse for the Beacon Street Girls.

#3 Letters from the Heart   ☐ **READ IT!**
Life seems perfect for Maeve and Avery . . . until they find out that in
seventh grade, the world can turn upside down just like that.

#4 Out of Bounds   ☐ **READ IT!**
Can the Beacon Street Girls bring the house down at Abigail Adams Junior
High's Talent Show? Or will the Queens of Mean steal the show?

#5 Promises, Promises   ☐ **READ IT!**
Tensions rise when two BSG find themselves in a tight race for seventh-
grade president at Abigail Adams Junior High.

#6 Lake Rescue   ☐ **READ IT!**
The seventh grade outdoor trip promises lots o' fun for the BSG—but will the
adventure prove too much for one sensitive classmate?

#7 Freaked Out   ☐ **READ IT!**
The party of the year is just around the corner. What happens when the
party invitations are given out . . . but not to everyone?

#8 Lucky Charm   ☐ **READ IT!**
Marty is missing! The BSG's frantic search for their beloved pup leads them to
a very famous person and the game of a lifetime.

#9 Fashion Frenzy   ☐ **READ IT!**
Katani and Maeve are off to the Big Apple for a supercool teen fashion
show. Will tempers fray in close quarters?

#10 Just Kidding   ☐ **READ IT!**
The BSG are looking forward to Spirit Week at Abigail Adams Junior High, until
some mean—and untrue—gossip about Isabel dampens everyone's spirits.

#11 Ghost Town
The BSG's fun-filled week at a Montana dude ranch includes skiing, snow boarding, cowboys, and celebrity twins—plus a ghost town full of secrets.

#12 Time's Up
Katani knows she can win the business contest. But with school and friends and family taking up all her time, has she gotten in over her head?

#13 Green Algae and Bubble Gum Wars
Inspired by the Sally Ride Science Fair, the BSG go green, but getting stuck slimed by some gooey supergum proves to be a major annoyance!

#14 Crush Alert
Romantic triangles and confusion abound as the BSG look forward to the Abigail Adams Junior High Valentine's Day dance.

#15 The Great Scavenger Hunt
Winning an ocean-side scavenger hunt isn't nearly as exciting for some of the BSG as surfing and beach volleyball or the chance to fulfill a Hollywood dream—with pirates!

#16 Sweet Thirteen
When Sophie comes to visit from Paris, French-mania sweeps through AAJH. Is Charlotte's fashionable friend too cool for her? Meanwhile, there's serious trouble with Maeve's thirteenth birthday bash. Can the BSG and Sophie save the day?

Also . . . Our Special Adventure Series:

Charlotte in Paris
Something mysterious happens when Charlotte returns to Paris to search for her long-lost cat and to visit her best Parisian friend, Sophie.

Maeve on the Red Carpet
A cool film camp at the Movie House is a chance for Maeve to become a star, but newfound fame has a downside for the perky redhead.

Freestyle with Avery
Avery Madden can't wait to go to Telluride, Colorado, to visit her dad! But there's one surprise that Avery's definitely not expecting.

Katani's Jamaican Holiday
A lost necklace and a plot to sabotage her family's business threaten to turn Katani's dream beach vacation in Jamaica into stormy weather.

Isabel's Texas Two-Step
A disastrous accident with a valuable work of art and a sister with a diva attitude give Isabel a bad case of the ups and downs on a special family trip.

Ready! Set! Hawaii!
Bon voyage! Pirates and parrots and an unwelcome surprise for Avery add complications and excitement to the BSG's dream vacation on a Hawaiian cruise.

FREE Club for you and your BFFs on BeaconStreetGirls.com!

If you loved this book, you'll love hanging out with the **Beacon Street Girls** (BSG)! **Join the BSG** (and their dog Marty) for virtual sleepovers, fashion tips, celeb interviews, games and more!

And with **Marty's secret code** (below), start getting **totally free stuff right away!** 🐾

To get **$5** in **MARTY $ MONEY** (one per person) go to **www.BeaconStreetGirls.com/redeem** and follow the instructions, while supplies last.

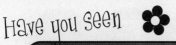

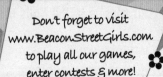